D0861722

TAXIMAN

TAXIMAN

Stories and Anecdotes from the Back Seat

BY
STANLEY PÉAN

Translated by David Homel

Prepared for the press by Linda Leith
Cover photo by Stephane Lavoie
Cover design by Debbie Geltner
Book design by Tika eBooks

Library and Archives Canada Cataloguing in Publication

Péan, Stanley, 1966-
[Taximan. English]
        Taximan : stories and anecdotes from the back seat / Stanley
Péan ; translated by David Homel.

Translation of: Taximan, propos et anecdotes recueillis depuis la banquette
arrière.

Issued in print and electronic formats.
ISBN 978-1-988130-89-7 (softcover).--ISBN 978-1-988130-90-3 (HTML).--
ISBN 978-1-988130-91-0 (HTML).--ISBN 978-1-988130-92-7 (PDF)

        1. Péan, Stanley, 1966- --Anecdotes. 2. Taxicabs--Anecdotes. 3.
Taxicab drivers--Anecdotes. 4. Haiti--Anecdotes. 5. Montréal (Québec)-
-Anecdotes. I. Homel, David. translator II. Title. III. Title: Taximan. English.

PS8581.E24T3913 2018   C848'.5403   C2018-901278-1
                            C2018-901279-X

Printed and bound in Canada.

The publisher gratefully acknowledges the support of the Government of
Canada through the Canada Council for the Arts, the Canada Book Fund,
and Livres Canada Books, and of the Government of Quebec through the
Société de développement des entreprises culturelles (SODEC).

We acknowledge the financial support of the Government of Canada
through the National Translation Program for Book Publishing, an initiative
of the *Roadmap for Canada's Official Languages 2013-2018: Education, Immigration, Communities*, for our translation activities.

Linda Leith Publishing
Montreal
www.lindaleith.com

For my father Maurice,
thirty-one years already…

And for the men and women
who work in the taxi industry,
who travel the avenues of life night and day

When cars start thinking,
the Rolls-Royce will be more anxious than the taxi cab.

—Henri Michaux

It's too bad that everyone who knows how to run a
country is busy driving taxis and cutting hair.

—George Burns

Where To?

Taxis have always been a great way to discover a city and its people, and taxi drivers have often been considered as philosophers, storytellers, and sociologists—with a little bit of psychopath thrown in from time to time. On these rides that you are about to take, not only do you get a classic set of drivers, but you will be accompanied by a perspicacious and sharp-eyed passenger, the writer and broadcaster Stanley Péan, one of Montreal's major voices.

Péan is something of a paradox. A man given to melancholy at times, he is also intensely social and has a good sense of the details that distinguish us as human beings. Best of all, he is equipped with a sense of humour about himself, and that is clear as he travels through the identity jungle of today's Montreal and elsewhere. Numerous are the Haitian drivers who insist that he is, despite all appearances, a white man, something that no one would normally think, let alone say. Instead of acting offended or accusing the drivers of illogical thinking or outright blindness, Péan investigates exactly what that comment means in the place where it has been spoken. In other words, *what am I?* And who are the others and what are their expectations of me? And how does my identity change as I move through my day?

As we ride through Montreal—though the scene does shift at times, moving all the way to Paris, then Ottawa, the Saguenay region, and Quebec City—we are not only travelling through space, but time. *Taximan* is a journey through the political and social landscape of the last few decades. Remember the Charlottetown Accord? Well, I had forgotten all about it too. But at one point it seemed as though the future of Canada was once again hanging in the balance. And the various taximen (as they are called in these pages) necessarily have their opinion or, in the opposite case, avoid forming any thoughts about the future of Canada at all. All citizens are supposed to know where they were on the morning September 11th, 2001, and Stanley Péan is no exception: he was in a taxi. Just as devastating for the people of Haiti, and Canadians of Haitian origin, was the January 2010 earthquake. These and other events are on the lips of the drivers and the reporters on their car radios.

These short sketches are meant to be just that, quick encounters, telling anecdotes, wisdom, or sometimes idiocy, from the mouths of strangers. But behind the charming aspect of these snapshots, there is plenty going on. The critique of tropical machismo and everyday racism, the never-ending dance between father and son and the easy tenderness a man feels for his mother, the immigrants' dilemma—should I stay or should I go?—the shifting identities that exist in any society, the precarious nature of many of its citizens … all this and more in a quick taxi ride. Often accompanied by *konpa dirèk*, that popular Haitian music that ends up torturing the ears of anyone who has ever taken a long bus ride in that country.

Music plays a major role on these rides, and no wonder, because Stanley Péan has been embellishing the national airwaves for the last number of years with his show "Quand le jazz est là" every weekday evening on Radio-Canada's *Ici Musique*. At one point, being something of a star host, he got his likeness on an immense billboard on the approach to the Champlain Bridge. Music is as much a minefield with taxi drivers as politics, and actually, the two are very much related.

I doubt whether many Canadians know about the enigmatic nature of Haitian immigration to this country. In fact, it was no immigration at all. It was recruitment, and Péan's father Maurice, we learn early on, was one of those men brought to Quebec. It was an offer not to be refused. He and his family would be saved from the Duvalier dictatorship, and in return, he would help modernize Quebec society at the beginnings of the Quiet Revolution, and in very elegant, *soigné* French. Representatives of the Quebec government's education ministry travelled to Haiti and skimmed off the cream of that society, the elites, who grasped the chance to exit the horrors of the dictatorship, though as every immigrant knows, the nostalgia that comes from leaving one's country follows a person all through his or her life.

Stanley Péan's *Taximan* is the trace, the record of that

exile. It is also a portrait of urban North America through its displaced people who, despite their native sadness, turn up the music and drive.

David Homel

Hop in!

A few years back, to help out a friend from Quebec City who was working in computer graphics, I agreed to deliver, in person, the proofs of a book to a Montreal publisher whom I happened to know. With his natural dry humour, the publisher greeted me in his stentorian voice by telling his receptionist, when she announced my presence, "I told you I don't want people sending me proofs by taxi. Quebec City to Montreal—can you imagine how much that cost?"

His joke was based on the large percentage of Haitians among Montreal taxi drivers, which has convinced more than one racist that a Haitian, or any other Black for that matter, could not possibly have another profession. My publisher friend probably did not realize that many Haitian cab drivers hold university diplomas, and that useless bureaucratic complications prevent their credentials from being recognized in their particular areas of expertise. But that prejudice, like all the others, seems unlikely to fade away, and hence his little joke when he saw me, package in hand, in the lobby of his publishing company.

If you're a Haitian, you must be a *taximan*, right? The word itself is a gift to us from colonial French.

In my case, that cliché is particularly incongruous, and you will allow me to explain the reason why with a little confession, scarcely conceivable in these times when a man's virility is linked to the type of automobile he drives: I don't have a driver's license, and I never learned to drive. I can't even tell you why I never got around to learning. That's just the way it is. And so, when I need to move around town, sometimes I use public transit, but most of the time I take a cab.

I have no idea of the enormous sums of money I have spent on taxi rides over the last thirty years. No doubt, for the morale of my budget, it's better if the amount remains unknown. People have given me the reputation as a big spender, a lavish sort of guy, and it's true, though I know that a taxi fare is not money foolishly spent. Over the years, I have noted down in memory the exchanges, some laconic, others stormy, that I have had with taxi drivers. For years, those men and women—and there a number of women drivers—have become familiar acquaintances, and we have discussed any number of subjects of common interest.

In Montreal, where Haitians make up a big part of the taxi industry, I'm always happy to fraternize with a small number of drivers who count me among their regular customers and speak to me in Creole. More than my family or friends, descendants of Haitian immigration as I am, the drivers are my most trustworthy link to the large

Haitian community in Quebec—and to my native country as well.

And so the idea of this collection came to me, a book inspired by stories I've heard and anecdotes I've experienced in the back seat of these vehicles. I have designed it as a series of telegraphic flashes, an informal anthology of sketches drawn in the heat of the action, the beginning of reflections that are never longer than the taxi ride that set them in motion in the first place.

But enough introduction: the meter is running.

So hop in and take a ride!

★

I have told this story before. Since it is just about as old as I am, I beg your indulgence if my memory of it is not perfectly faithful to the reality of all its details.

It is November 1966. My father, whom we called Mèt Mo (from "maître," the honorary title for lawyers, which he was, and "Mo" for Maurice), had just arrived in Jonquière, Quebec, from Haiti, and there he met a man, a friendly sort of guy with whom he conversed a moment or two in a bus or a train, who knows which. I can imagine the subjects of conversation: the perpetual tragedy of Haitian politics, the harsh Quebec winters, the labyrinths of different accents... The usual nonsense.

Mèt Mo and the man said goodbye in amiable fashion. And then, considering how small Jonquière is, they were destined to meet several months later, in the gentleman's taxi. The driver recognized his exotic passenger from their last encounter, and quickly began asking after his family, his new life, and all the rest, and inquired whether my father had found work. Mèt Mo answered, By all means, at the Guillaume-Tremblay Secondary School, which has since been renamed the École polyvalente d'Arvida. Delighted, the man asked him if he was working as a cook in the cafeteria.

"Unfortunately, no," my father replied, putting on a disappointed countenance. "I would have liked to, but there was nothing available. I had to settle for being a French teacher."

★

"Your face reminds me of someone. You wouldn't be…?" the driver asked me, a Haitian in his fifties with greying hair.

With some apprehension, I waited for the rest of the question. I have heard it often over the years. At the supermarket check-out, in a taxi (even from Haitian drivers), and elsewhere.

Let me think… The first time, and the most terrible time it happened to me, was at the Saguenay Salon du Livre, a regional book fair held at the Jonquière Polyvalente in the fall of 1989. I had been invited to talk about my first book, *La plage des songes*. My friend, the writer and TV journalist Dany Laferrière, was also in attendance. He had just stepped down from the stage where he had participated in a panel discussion and was walking toward me. We spoke briefly, then both moved on to what we had to do next.

A couple minutes later, a lady came up to me and asked me if I had just been on stage.

The same thing happened the next day, a few minutes before the closing ceremonies. The organizers were jubilant: it had been a great event with record-breaking crowds. I was chatting with a friend of my brother Reynald when suddenly a lady volunteer from the organization rushed up to me. She was the one who had given me my badge identifying me as Stanley Péan, which I was still clearly wearing. She wanted to thank me for taking the trouble to attend the fair, congratulated me on my book, and encouraged me to keep on with "my extraordinary work on television!"

My jaw dropped. The lady was certain she had just had a conversation with Dany Laferrière. No one was going to tell her that was impossible, that Dany had taken a plane to Montreal, that he had left that morning and so she couldn't have met him that afternoon. For her, I was Dany Laferrière.

At the Quebec City Salon du Livre, at some later date, I was talking with my friend Anne Dandurand. A woman working at a booth called out to Anne, telling her she very much appreciated her novel *Un coeur qui craque*, and wondered whether Anne had another project on the go—the usual thing. Then she turned in my direction and asked if by chance I hadn't published something too.

I decided to make a preemptive strike.

"Yes, a collection of short stories. *La plage des songes*, written by Stanley Péan."

The woman was unstoppable. She listened to my answer with an affable smile, she told me that was interesting, but...

"And that other one, the guy who wrote *How to Make Love to a Black Person* [sic], what's his name?"

The variations on this little story could go on forever, but I think I'll stop here. The Other One. Okay, let's say that all Black men look alike—sometimes I even think my reflection in the mirror belongs to someone else—but there are limits, aren't there?

If this keeps on, I'll end up paranoid. When strangers approach me, I will begin to doubt they are really talking to me. I have fallen into an episode of *The Twilight Zone*. When you think about it, Quebec has way more Black writers than Dany and me, and way more Blacks too, for that matter.

Whether anyone is listening or not, I'll shout it out again, "No, I'm not Dany Laferrière!"

We don't even belong to the same family. All right, we were both born in Haiti, but his family is from Petit-Goâve and mine from Cap-Haïtien. Maybe someone could mix us up in Montreal or Quebec City. But at the Jonquière secondary school, my alma mater, the very school where for years my father was the terror of every student, the school where I was the editor of the newspaper and the president of the student council? I protest! I'd rather have the label "Raynald's brother" or "Steve's brother."

Hear this, once and for all: I am not Dany Laferrière. And if ever we cross paths, don't come and ask me about the screenplay for *How to Make Love to Two Negroes and Tell Them Apart*!

The driver completed his sentence, pulling me from my reverie.

"You wouldn't be Stanley Péan, the writer and journalist?"

Our eyes met in the rear-view mirror. With a silly

13

smile, I nodded, thinking that one day someone might ask Dany Laferrière if he'd ever been challenged with the same question.

That would be balm for my sense of self.

★

"*Ban'm zen an, non...*

More than an invitation, it was an order. Haitian taxi-men often serve it up to me once they identify me. Despite all these years in Montreal, I admit I'm still a little taken aback when someone addresses me in Creole. In our family, when my cousin Joëlle and my brother Raynald and I were kids, my father forbade us to speak Creole, even if the language came naturally to him when he spoke to my mother. Did he really think we didn't understand a single word? Whatever his reasons, he insisted we speak the language of Molière before venturing into the territory used by Languichatte, the popular Haitian tale-teller.

As I left my teenage years behind, I began answering my father's comments and my Uncle Émile's questions (my father's brother) in Creole, and then started inserting whole passages of that language into my early short stories. That practice earned me my father's disapproval, which he expressed with a very Haitian *tchuip*—that most Creole onomatopoeia that communicates disgust, dismay, or disappointment.

"*Ti gason, sispann ranse, non: pou ki sa ou kwè fò w pale kreyòl, ou ki pa menm ayisyen vre?*" my father would inevitably retort, obviously trying to wound my pride. Why do you feel you have to speak Creole when you're not even really Haitian?

The driver was waiting for my answer. I translated mentally: *ban'm zen a*, tell me the news, the latest gossip, the latest rumour. With pleasure. But first I had to decide which story might titillate my partner in conversation.

"*Ki zen ou bezwen tande, mon chè?*" I answer sometimes, just to stall for time, which rarely gains the driver's favour. In other words, What gossip do you want to hear?

As in my father's house, I heard a well-rounded *tchuip*, the sign of disappointment.

"*Ah, ou pas ayisyen vre,*" he deduced—you're not a real Haitian.

Okay, I'm not an authentic Haitian. So be it. But can someone tell me how true Haitianness is measured?

When someone asks me where I'm from, I always hesitate. Born in Port-au-Prince, I spent my entire childhood in Jonquière, in the Saguenay region of Quebec, where my parents settled the year I was born. That makes me a Québécois, but with roots in another country I have learned about through other people's memories. Haitian by blood, but raised in a milieu radically different from the land of my ancestors. Québécois and Haitian, then, both one and the other, yet neither one nor the other.

In the middle of the 1970s, the Péans "had themselves built something," as they say in the Saguenay, in the housing development that was springing up in what used to be the vast fields that once belonged to Old Man Gagnon, a farmer and landowner. My family had left Haiti ten years earlier, and the purchase of a house represented, in a very real way, a sign of resignation. They would not be returning home any time soon.

The little bungalow on rue de la Tamise sheltered my father Maurice, my mother Irène, their five children, and my niece Joëlle; her mother had entrusted her to us when she was born. Like most first-wave Haitian immigrants, my parents belonged to the privileged class of their native society who had fled the terror of the Papa Doc Duvalier's dictatorship.

For years, my father harboured bitter memories of a conversation with Luc Désir, Papa Doc's devoted lieutenant and éminence grise of the Tontons Macoutes, the hated secret police. The conversation, if it could be called that, ended in blows. My father never seemed to me so bitter as when he recalled, teeth clenched, holding back his hatred, that man whom he rightly considered a mad dog.

The son of a magistrate from Cap-Haïtien on the north coast of the country, educated as a lawyer, Mèt Mo was able to continue his studies at the famed École nationale d'administration in Paris, courtesy of a substantial UNESCO scholarship. Up until her passing, my mother, Lady I., as her sister Michèle called her, would recall that year she spent with him in the City of Light, and she would make us laugh till we cried with her stories about Maurice in gentle, civilized France, back when Paris could lay claim to being the capital of the world. For example, one morning in a café, the *garçon* watched in horror as Maurice added one, two, then three cubes of sugar to his espresso. Seeing his incredulous look, Maurice said to the young Frenchman, "You know, don't you, that this stuff comes from my country."

After several years of working for the government of Paul Eugène Magloire as a senior civil servant, my father went on to build a career in French-language education in Port-au-Prince after the fall of the Magloire regime, and he continued in that vein in Jonquière.

In those days, and it is still the case today, Blacks were rare in the Saguenay Lac Saint-Jean region, in northeastern Quebec. At most, there must have been a dozen Haitian households scattered across the territory: the Cadets, the Dauphins, the Kavanaghs, the Mathieus, the Mételluses, the Norrises ... and the Péans as well, who lived in three different spots in Jonquière and Kénogami. Do you remember that federal minister by the name of Benoît Bouchard who one day congratulated himself in the Commons on the fact that, contrary to Montreal, his region had not been "bothered" by immigration? When you come down to it, my family constituted the entire Haitian community in our little town. You can imagine how difficult it would have been to start a gang of teenage delinquents or even a street demonstration.

I grew up in a subdivision atmosphere in this small provincial city, and several times a day I made the trip between the Little Haiti of our modest bungalow, and the white bread Quebec society that had taken us in—and I never had to show a passport!

These days in Montreal, sometimes the cops stop me for having crossed a deserted street without waiting for the light to change... in other words, for walking while Black. Make no mistake, I can distinguish between policemen, most of whom are good enough guys, and the minority in the force, those cops who turn their guns on a young Black man who isn't even armed, and whose crime is to vaguely resemble a composite sketch of a wanted criminal, or not to have paid his taxi fare.

★

Under a hot sun, Black teenagers dressed in hip-hop style are hanging out on boulevard Saint-Michel, gathered in groups between the pizzerias selling a slice for a dollar, and the convenience stores that feature Cola Couronne and other sugary tropical delicacies, as a parade of ebony Lolitas streams by.

"*Nou rive, wi, mèt!*" the driver announces as he pulls over.

Arrival at destination.

I didn't have to give him the exact address of the Maison d'Haïti. Whether or not he lives in the Saint-Michel neighbourhood, every Haitian taximan worth his salt can find this beacon of community life without a GPS. In this district, there are some 16,000 residents of Haitian origin. The sector isn't where you find the greatest numbers—there are double that number in Park Extension-Rosemont—but Saint-Michel boasts the highest density of Haitians in Montreal. Nearly half the students in the neighbourhood schools are born of parents from that island, where "Negritude stood tall for the first time," in the masterful words of the poet Aimé Césaire.

"*Twòp vagabondaj nan lari a!*" the driver fumes.

Too much hanging around the streets! Those words echo the recriminations heard everywhere the Haitian diaspora has settled over the last forty years. One fine Friday afternoon, because of a wave of crimes committed by young Haitians, the police reacted by arresting every young Black male in the Saint-Michel subway station at rush hour. Operation Blackfly—that was the name given the operation—provoked the anger of the community, especially since out of the seventy individuals charged, only a dozen had actually any gang involvement.

Like many compatriots of his generation, who did not believe they were immigrating for good, my taxi driver feels a certain dismay toward these young people who seem to have rejected traditional Haitian culture and who are scarcely recognizable in the street, so completely have they assimilated the fashions and models of US hip-hop.

"Even their Creole isn't real Creole, my friend!" he exclaimed as he launched into what was obviously a favourite subject. "They talk a kind of dialect, a stinking stew of Creole, English, and bad Quebec French."

I find the elders' astonished disapproval of young people more than exasperating. You don't have to be a sociologist to understand the effects of immigration on the transmission of the original culture.

In an article I published a few years ago, I tried to draw a portrait of Haitian Quebec culture, born of a mixing of influences and roots, and I situated it somewhere between the voodoo rhythms of *rada* and rap, between *soup joumou*—the traditional squash soup my father would make for New Year's Day—and the meat pies of Lac Saint-Jean and the McDonald's version of poutine. Between Creole,

English, and the Quebec French that the elders hold in such contempt, with all their open-mouthed admiration of France. Haitian Quebec culture, like the music of the rap group Muzion, has its roots firmly anchored in the province's pluri-ethnic landscape.

But this is no time for popular sociology. I have come to interview a Haitian social worker who has set up a neighbourhood patrol of young people who walk the streets of the district and exhort their brothers and sisters not to commit any regrettable acts that might earn them a free trip to the police station.

★

This little story always makes me smile. Sometimes I tell it to young readers to illustrate how seemingly ordinary events can make their way into books.

I was in Ottawa, spending three days as part of a Canada Council literary jury. It was my last trip to the region for the year, the last of three, and my final opportunity to do a little research on the local colour I absolutely needed for a sequence in my novel *Zombi Blues* that takes place across the river in Hull—which was the name by which the city of Gatineau was still known, back then.

"Do you have any plans for the evening?" asked the lady friend with whom I was having dinner in a decent steak house near the Parliament.

"Yes. I need to go visit a cemetery. Care to come with me?"

Needless to say, my companion turned down my invitation.

I couldn't blame her. We went our separate ways after dinner. It was eleven o'clock at night. I went up to my room to grab my notebook, then took the elevator back down and jumped into one of the taxis parked in front of the hotel.

"Where to, sir?"

"Do you know Hull?" I asked him.

"Hull? Of course, I know Hull. Right across the river."

Yes, I knew that much too. Judging by his dark skin and accent, I figured the driver was a recent immigrant, probably from Turkey or Pakistan. Daniel, a friend from college from Jonquière whom I'd had a beer with the evening before, in memory of the good old days, told me there was a cemetery in Hull, more or less facing my hotel, but on the Quebec side of the Ottawa River. The place seemed like the perfect spot to bury the character whose funeral launches the novel.

"I'm asking you how well you know Hull because I need to go to the cemetery on boulevard Taché."

My driver looked surprised, and suspicious.

"Cemetery?"

There's one thing I have learned about Ottawa, the capital of the country that Pierre Elliott Trudeau dreamed of being bilingual "from one Atlantic to the other," as Jean Chrétien would say, and that's that you have to do like in Rome: adopt the local customs and ways of speaking. My father Mèt Mo had a proverb and a saying for every occasion, and he would have trotted out this one now: "*si'w vle ale nan veye koukou.*" If you want to go to a party with the cuckoos, you'd better be ready to eat horse droppings.

"Yes. The cemetery."

"Cemetery?"

There was one small problem: my travelling companion's English was as rudimentary as his French, and neither "cemetery" nor "graveyard" set off any familiar echoes for him. We were crossing the bridge over the Ottawa River that stretched out below like a flowing satin sheet.

"Graveyard? Is that the name of a bar?"

"No. It's a place where you bury dead people."

"Dead people?"

Since I didn't feel like driving around in circles all night and paying for it, I recommended he call his dispatcher and ask for directions. Sure enough, I heard a voice tell him he would find the cemetery on boulevard Taché just before reaching the Champlain Bridge.

"Champlain Bridge! I know Champlain Bridge!" he said triumphantly, eager to reassure me.

Yet, as we drove along boulevard Taché in the supposed right direction, we came to the Champlain Bridge without seeing any sign of the cemetery. I told the driver to stop at the first convenience store, and I got out to ask directions.

The woman at the cash let me know in a friendly enough fashion that I'd gone right by the place. How could I have missed it? Easy: my friend Daniel had told me that you couldn't see the river from the cemetery, so I'd kept my eyes on the right side of the boulevard, whereas the cemetery lay to the left, by the fire station.

Back in the taxi, I told my driver as much.

"Fire station! I know fire station!"

And we turned back the other way.

"There it is!" I exclaimed a minute later, like a sailor

spotting land on the horizon after months at sea—and I'm only exaggerating a little.

As I pointed to the wide stretch of land dotted with gravestones and encircled by dense woods, the driver finally understood what my destination was. To say he was surprised was putting it mildly. He clearly had little experience in dropping off passengers in a cemetery on a Friday evening around midnight.

I handed him a twenty-dollar bill, took the change in return, and stepped out. He looked uncertain; should he wait for me? I told him not to bother.

"Have a good evening, sir," he stammered, not knowing what to think.

Obviously, he had no experience with the research methods writers use.

★

Fresh off the Quebec City bus, I climbed into the back-seat of the car and told the driver my destination. It was late and I wasn't in the mood for idle chatter. Good thing, because the driver, a Haitian my age or so, was too caught up in his phone conversation to pay me any mind. He turned left onto Saint-Hubert and moved up the hill to the Plateau neighbourhood, talking away to his invisible partner in conversation.

Despite the late hour, a CD was playing full blast, and I thought I recognized the artist, Sweet Mickey. I was sure it was him. And considering what happened next, I'd like to state here and now that the song was *Pa manyen fanm la konsa*, but that would be too good a coincidence, and people would say I was tinkering with reality. You see, the title, which literally means "You shouldn't put your hands all over that woman that way," is a humorous take on trying to seduce a woman who is already taken, and the tune is the same as Cesaria Evora's "Angola."

I was exhausted, all I could think of was sleep, yet I couldn't help following my driver's side of the conversation. He must have figured I neither spoke nor understood Creole, and that I wasn't even Haitian. What other explanation was there for his complete lack of discretion?

The subject was his women—he had several, that

much was obvious, which confirmed the well-worn cliché about Haitian machismo, either real or presumed. From what I understood from his exclamations, he was angry at one of his friends who clearly had no luck with the fair sex, and to whom he had apparently lent one of his lovers out of sheer compassion. It seemed that the beneficiary's behaviour with the young lady in question fell far short of my driver's expectations.

"*Ou imagine w: se fanm pa m mwen ba li e msye al fè malònèt avè l!*" he exclaimed. "*Fanm pa m, wi!*"

From what I understood, he had given one of his women to his friend, who had acted like a cad with her. Imagine—one of his women!

I had to smile. The way his friend acted brought to mind a saying from my neck of the woods: don't expect a pig to thank you for giving him dinner.

★

You won't see the two of them on TV, and you won't recognize their names either. Yet at the time their point of view seemed to me at least as interesting as anything Pierre Elliott Trudeau could have come up with... or Céline Dion, for that matter.

The first guy was a dyed-in-the wool Quebecker who had come to pick me up at my mother's house in Quebec City, for I had to return to Montreal for an emergency. Between the Parc des Braves and Central Station, very quickly he exhausted all the usual refrains (the endless rainy days, the summer that really wasn't one, etc.), so he had to start improvising. To do this, we used the call and response model from gospel music: what did I do for a living, and did I plan on going back to my country (in Africa, he thought!) when I finished my studies here.

Don't ask why, but I decided to play the game. I conjured up my beloved and faraway Abidjan, and the professor's job that I would return to once I had earned my doctorate. This scene took place way back in the fall of 1992. The radio was talking non-stop about the "Wilhelmy Affair," and its possible repercussions on the Charlottetown Accord.

For those who have forgotten all about those days, in the fall of October 1992, a few hours after the end of the

Charlottetown negotiations during which the provincial premiers had come to an agreement about the Constitution that was to be submitted to a referendum, the media got a hold of an intercepted cell phone conversation between lawyer André Tremblay—an expert in constitutional law and minister Gil Rémillard's right-hand man—and Diane Wilhelmy, Quebec's Deputy Minister of Intergovernmental Affairs, who had not attended the meetings because of ill health. Initially forbidden from publication, the recording featured the two high-level civil servants criticizing premier Robert Bourassa's ineffective and weak style at the negotiating table, and the revelations had a devastating impact on the results of the vote on Charlottetown.

I decided to ask the driver for a few explanations about the constitutional swamp that the country was apparently bogged down in. Without necessarily returning all the way back to the Flood, he launched into a retrospective of the abuse perpetrated against Quebec by English Canada, thanks to the complicity of sell-outs like Bourassa, Mulroney, Chrétien, and company. A compressed history of Quebec in ten minutes, dynamic and animated: the Conscription Crisis, the occupation of October 1970, the federal side's political terrorism of 1980, the Repatriation of the Constitution, the Meech Lake Accord, the laughable martyrdom of Anglo-Quebeckers who, no matter what Mordecai Richler maintained, were the most coddled minority in the world—except for the Afrikaners, perhaps! Ever since Lord Durham, the driver declared, English

Canada has been running a stealth campaign to eliminate the *peuple québécois*.

We reached the station. As I pulled out my wallet, I reminded him, as the devil's advocate must do, that in Africa we too had believed independence would solve all our problems. Forty years later, we had to face the tragic facts of the situation...

As for the other guy, I met him the next day going in the opposite direction. Hailed on René-Lévesque West, going to the bus station on Berri, heading back to the capital city.

I couldn't lie about my origins to this Haitian taximan, especially since he had seen me on TV the evening before. His Jetta was swaying to the faithful rhythms of *konpa dirèk*, that popular Haitian standby, and not the national news on the radio, but a copy of *La Presse* was lying on the back seat with its headline about the referendum. This opened a door for me to move the subject of conversation in a more local direction, since up until then it had been centered on Haitian President Aristide's unlikely return to power, now that he had been toppled by Cédras the year before.

The rear-view mirror reflected the surprise on the driver's face. The guy had absolutely no answer. I pushed him. He'd been living here for fifteen or twenty years—it was impossible he would have no opinion on the Quebec-Canada issue. He ended up capitulating. He had come here with their two daughters, he and his wife had known the purgatory of being cheap labour in the factories, which were preferable to Duvalier's inferno, but certainly not anything like paradise. Things had improved since then. His wife had a more humane schedule and was making a more decent rate of pay, and one of his daughters would soon be starting university.

Gone was the anxiety at the prospect of being sent back to the country of the hated secret police, but now new worries were tormenting him, and he had begun wondering whether he shouldn't consider going home. Why? Didn't he feel any sense of belonging in Quebec? The hope of Canada's economic stability had attracted him here, that was nearly thirty years ago, he said, though he had voted Yes in the 1980 Referendum because the movement of those Quebec citizens who had welcomed him seemed legitimate. But today, with all these right-wing extremists who called for a sovereign, white Quebec....

Don't mix up nationalism and racism, I objected. He told me that in Haiti, slogans about national pride helped bring Papa Doc to power. The rise of the far right and neo-Nazism, I reminded him, wasn't limited to Quebec and was surely not linked to Canada's constitutional destiny. He admitted I was right, but added that the issue didn't concern him, and that he wasn't going to vote. When it came to sovereignty, he would rather go back to his country, and if he was killed by a Macoute, the secret police, at least it would be one of his own kind.

Disproving the myth according to which Haitian drivers always try to rip off their customers, we reached the

Berri bus station with no suspicious detours. As he took the tip I added to the fare, he congratulated me for my success (the poor guy never saw my sales reports!), then added a good-hearted *Kenbe pa lage, mèt!* – Hold the fort, brother.

Later, uncomfortably wedged in between the arm-rests of a seat in a bus speeding down Highway 20, I thought back to the two men. Time had proven Hugh MacLennan wrong. Canada is not made up of two solitudes, but a multitude that follow their separate ways through the body politic, and will never meet.

★

The guy wasn't Haitian, even if he said he was. After greeting me with a salvo of jokes and puns, he asked me where I was from. And once he received his answer, he offered this confession that was surprising to say the least.

"I have a Haitian passport, you know," he told me in an accent I couldn't quite identify. "If you don't believe me, I'll show you."

Don't bother. I wasn't some sort of Doubting Thomas who had to stick his fingers in the wound in the Saviour's side. Still, his claim demanded some sort of explanation. Full of facetious banter, the man delivered the goods.

"Twenty years ago, I spent some time in Jacmel, more than one stay. I left Poland long before that, and I used to vacation in your country."

What was he talking about? It was "our" country, since he claimed it was his too. But I didn't dare interrupt his nostalgic soliloquy about the beauties of René Depestre's native town, especially since the place fascinated me too. The majestic mountains. The salty air. The splendour of the women. But he wasn't some sort of Club Med brochure. The man had immersed himself in the local culture, and was close to people there. I didn't have to wait long to hear the reasons behind his naturalization.

"It's a little known historical fact. A great majority, if not all of the Polish soldiers who were conscripts in the troops sent to Haiti by Napoleon to put down the Haitian uprising changed sides once they arrived there."

I remembered having read about that episode in a Roger Dorsinville novel. After Haiti declared its independence, the Poles were the only Whites to enjoy a warm reception on the territory of the former colony of Saint-Domingue, and Poland became the official backer of the new republic. The descendants of those soldiers were scattered among villages perched on the tops of tall mountains, and difficult to reach. Even today, you could find cemeteries whose gravestones revealed Polish-sounding names.

"In case you didn't know, it is written in the constitution that any Pole who wishes to acquire Haitian citizenship just has to ask for it, it's a mere formality," my driver informed me. "So once, during one of my stays, I made my request."

Really, that tragic half of an island would never cease to astonish me. But the man hadn't finished his story.

"I must admit, I had *yon menaj* there, as you put it," he added, his eyes sparkling with laughter.

Yon menaj—I should have suspected. A girlfriend. *Cherchez la femme*, as the Americans say. He was out to marry Haiti. But then I remembered: he had spoken in the past tense.

"Did you get married in Haiti?"

"Not all the way, but almost. She was so beautiful, we

38

loved each other so much, I spent all my time with her. I was about to begin the process to bring her back to Canada. But when I returned to Jacmel a few months later, I discovered she was pregnant."

"By you?"

"No. It was her ex-boyfriend's. The truth is, she was already pregnant when we met, but she didn't tell me. By the time I went back, she'd reached the point where she couldn't hide it anymore. She told me that she and the father had reconciled when I was away, and they'd decided to raise the child together. She had tears in her eyes. I think she really loved me."

"And so you left."

"Yes, broken-hearted," he said, a ghost of a smile playing on his lips.

"And you never returned?"

"Never. What would be the point? I'd lost the woman I loved."

He paused, then added in a confidential tone, "You know, the worst thing is that once you've tasted the pleasures of Creole women, it's not easy going back to the White ones... "

What do you know, here was another variation on "Once you go Black, you never come back." The man smiled at me again in his rear-view mirror.

"That's why I ended up marrying an enchanting Thai woman."

The story ended happily ever after. He had photos of his lovely wife in a bikini on a beach somewhere, and he showed them to me as if they were the elements of proof I could place in his file.

★

I had to yank on the handle to make sure the door was safely closed. There—done. I told the driver my destination.

"Ah, you're heading up North," he commented.

North is relative, but it's always good to know which way is up. This little jaunt would take me from Pointe-Saint-Charles, the old industrial southwest district of Montreal, to the Plateau, central and chic. Hardly the far North.

"It's north of where we are now. But not the same north as in Haiti," I added.

And it's not the Saguenay either, I could have added.

"Ah, so you're Haitian."

"At the beginning, yes. How did you figure that out?"

"Your accent."

I raised an eyebrow. "Really? That's the first time I've heard that one."

It was his turn to be surprised.

"You're joking."

"Not at all. Most Haitian drivers accuse me of talking like a Quebecker."

"I can understand them," he said, nodding. "It's an accent I wouldn't wish on anyone, not even my worst enemy."

"You're exaggerating."

"Not at all. When I first came here, I had no idea what they were talking about, if anything."

The driver reminded me of my father's harsh judgements about language. When it came to his students in Jonquière, he made the same demands for linguistic correctness that he imposed on his children. I've heard that easy criticism all too often, the kind that flows from Parisian arrogance and produces results like the ones I've seen on French national television, when some eyewitness account from Marseille is subtitled, as if all other accents were treated as foreign languages.

"How long have you been in Quebec?"

"I came here ten years ago, dear sir," the driver told me. "Before that, I lived in Paris. For twenty years."

I could have told him I could tell by his accent, but I'll skip the easy targets.

"What part do you come from?" he asked.

"You mean Haiti, or Quebec?"

He let fly with an emphatic *tchuip*.

"Haiti, Haiti, what do you think, sir?"

"I was born in Port-au-Prince, but my family is from Cap-Haïtien."

"Ah, the Kingdom of the North, we're back there again. It's like a little Haiti within Haiti. Strange, though, you don't have the northern accent, or that of Port-au-Prince either."

"My parents moved to Jonquière when I was a baby."

"Jonquière? I've heard of it... It's in Lanaudière?"

42

"No, you're thinking of Joliette. Jonquière is in the Saguenay, two hours north by car from Quebec City. It's like a little Quebec within Quebec."

I wondered whether my father, proud native of Cap-Haïtien that he was, purposely chose to settle in this new Kingdom of the North, separated from the rest of the country by trackless forests, just as le Cap, as it is called back there, is cut off by a chain of high mountains. Some coincidences can't help but make you smile.

★

It's true, I plead guilty, I'm always on the lookout for odd stories, sometimes tragic, other times banal, all of which make up our existence. I'm more than just open to them—I seek them out. What could be more normal? All writers enjoy breaking into other people's secret gardens to pick some radiant flower—or some evil herb they can slip into their work that they build with every passing day. Writers are life-stealers, vampires.

But sometimes a taxi ride can take place in the grimmest of silences. No use lamenting, it's just that way. Once the destination has been announced, the car takes off without the slightest word between driver and passenger. The atmosphere depends on the disposition of each party, I suppose, a chemistry that does not kick in, or some unfathomable factor.

In which case the vampire goes hungry. He sits on the back seat, idly scanning the headlines of the paper next to him, watching the cityscape parade past, listening to his inner music, the blues refrain from the morning after.

And he thinks of his former sins.

★

I would be lying if I claimed that the Prince song about the lady cab driver, a combination of eroticism and humour, was playing on the radio when I settled onto the backseat. As charming as they may seem, such coincidences occur only in Paul Auster novels. That being said, when I recognized the *grimèl* behind the wheel—the Creole word for a light-skinned Black woman with Black facial features— I couldn't help recalling that track from the album *1999* that turned me into a fervent fan of His Purple Majesty from Minneapolis, back when I was a teenager, in another life. Like me, Prince climbed into a car piloted by a woman, and in his admitted state of confusion, all he wanted was to be taken for a ride.

Only a song, you say?

"Ah, hello, my heart, where have you been? And where do I take you today?"

True, it had been a while since I'd ridden with her or one of her sisters. In the Montreal taxi industry, women seem to be in the clear minority. If we are to believe the reportage done by Anne-Marie Provost, a colleague from Radio-Canada, and her broadcast for International Women's Day, the taxi business is still dominated by men. Of the 10,353 drivers in Montreal, only 125 are women.

No wonder I rarely get in a taxi and discover that a woman will be driving me through the streets of my city. One of them, an old-stock Quebec woman nearing sixty who used to take me regularly from the house where the mother of my children lived, in Pointe-de-Sainte-Foy, to downtown Quebec City, reminded me of one of my grade school teachers back in the Saguenay. Another, also a White Quebecker who would sometime pick me up in east-end Montreal, had an unusual second career. She was a real estate agent when she wasn't behind the wheel, and could not understand how I could refuse her offers of bargain condos that were perfect for a fashionable man of good taste (her words, not mine) like me. A third, an English speaker with a dark complexion, maybe Turkish or from the Middle East, never spoke a word to me, unless it was to criticize the chaotic and dangerous driving habits of city drivers.

And then there was this one. A stunning *métisse* with green eyes and a proud forehead, whose hairstyle made me think of the singer Sade. I don't believe she was Haitian—something, her accent, the way she formed her sentences and expressed herself, suggested origins elsewhere in the Antilles. I could have asked her the obvious question, you might say, but we never ventured into personal territory. Our talk was always light and easy, we engaged in soft courting with no intention of going further.

I told her where I was going; she started the engine and turned over the meter. I was swimming in waves of melancholy that afternoon, and flirting was not on my mind, even just for fun. She felt that immediately and spoke with a certain discretion.

"Troubles with your sweetheart, perhaps?"

What could I tell her? There wasn't any sweetheart anymore, she dropped me a while back—the story of my life, and I was not sure I wanted to compose an epilogue on the subject just then. The taxiwoman and I hardly knew each other. And yet… Over a period of years, when I rode in her car, most of the time I was alone, but other times with a friend, a lover, or a beloved. But it came back to me suddenly: one evening, my driver witnessed an acrimonious and rather theatrical argument between the now-extinguished flame and me.

I didn't know anything about my driver, and could not say whether these two children whose photos she kept on the passenger side visor were hers, her sister's, or a friend's. She wasn't wearing a ring on her finger, but that didn't mean she didn't have someone in her life. For years I have had intimate yet chaste relations with a number of women, and I know for a fact that true friendship is possible between a man and a woman, even if some alpha males don't think so. But what clues could you trust when it comes to imagining the sort of relationship you might have with a perfect stranger who drives you from point A to point B?

The greater part of the trip took place in total silence, contrary to our habit. The words of that Prince tune echoed in my ears. Were they a premonition? When she gave me my change, the lovely lady cab driver also slipped a scrap of paper into my hand. On it she had scrawled her phone number. "If ever you want to talk over a drink or a cup of coffee, some evening ..."

Her smile was a promise.

I never called her. I never came across her again. And I lost the fateful scrap of paper. An accident? I can be so disorganized. Who knows? Maybe she isn't behind the wheel anymore.

I will probably never know.

As I said, sometimes absolutely nothing happens during a ride. Or afterwards.

And then, to quote a good friend of mine, a writer, sometimes the best stories are when the boy does not get the girl ....

★

All right, I won't make a hard and fast rule, but from my observation, there are very few taximen who listen to classical music or even the middle-of-the-road stations. Very few tune into Radio-Canada, except when the international news comes on. The majority of men behind the wheel are plugged into Montreal's Haitian radio stations that play music from the Antilles, or shows hosted by preachers who promise their flock that their souls will be saved, or the phone-in shows that usually cover the latest political crisis back home, as is the case today.

I settled in and named my destination: Dorval Airport, that some time ago was renamed by Jean Chrétien for Pierre Elliott Trudeau, a complete aberration when you consider the controversial and not very bright decisions of the late chief of state concerning the development of air traffic in Montreal. The driver, a Haitian man not much older than me, offered to take a different route, but first I had to approve it. It was fine with me as long as I got where I had to be at the time I had to be there. The car pulled into the stream of traffic.

The way he chose was clearly the better option. So far, not a single traffic tie-up. If all went well, I'd be at the airport ahead of schedule.

"Are you flying back to Haiti?" he asked.

"No, just domestic. I'm going to Rouyn-Noranda, in the Abitibi. You know, for a book fair."

From the look on his face, you would have thought I was describing some distant spot in the heart of an impenetrable jungle. It's odd, but most of my fellow countrymen live like Montrealers, born and raised, with a total ignorance of the geography of the rest of the province. Island-dwellers, past and present—and future too, or so it seems.

"Have you not been home for a while?"

"It hasn't been so long," he told me. "I try to get back twice a year, at least."

"Do you still have a lot of family there?"

"Yes, but I don't go just to see them. It's important to recharge my batteries and stay in touch with myself. And what about you?"

"I have all sorts of aunts and uncles there. A lot of them lived overseas for most of their lives, but they've gone back for their retirement."

"Do you go back very often?"

"Not often. To tell the truth, I don't really know Haiti," I confessed, open-hearted. "I was born in Port-au-Prince, but my parents came here when I was a baby. I went back once when I was a child, and a couple times these last years."

"You're right. You don't really know Haiti."

On the radio, the host of the phone-in show and the listeners were debating the repatriation by the US Coast Guard of more than a hundred Haitian boat people to the small town of Bizoton, and the repatriation of several hundred more by the Bahamian government. The driver and I listened and interrupted the discussion with our own analysis. We agreed on one point: it was tragedy enough for these poor people to have to leave their country for economic reasons, but it was more tragic still for them to die on the open sea. But what explained the hypocrisy of those foreign governments that refused entry to these unfortunate people without taking time to wonder about the living conditions that incited them to embark on this exodus in leaky boats?

"When you think about George Bush's America, you can't be surprised," my driver stated. "But I'm a little disappointed by the Bahamas. Well, like we say back home, *depi lan Ginen nèg pa vle wè nèg*, I guess."

I studied proverbs under my father's tutelage, and I knew this one well: Ever since Guinea, that is, since the land of our ancestors, the great beyond where our Black souls will return after we die, the Black man has hated the Black man.

As a way of summing up two hundred years of tumultuous and often bloody political history, marked by a decolonization that has never truly succeeded, perpetual fratricidal warfare, and foreign intervention, for the most part covert, I found this proverb a little simplistic, a quick way out.

"I'm telling you, as soon as he has a chance, the Black man wastes no time stabbing his brother in the back," the driver pushed on, completely caught up in his own logic.

"That atavism explains why neither Aristide, nor anybody else, will ever be able to do anything good for the country in any lasting way."

"You're exaggerating. That's not the type of relationship I've had with the Blacks I know."

"That's normal, brother. You're not Black, you're White!" he laughed.

I had no reply. That one really shut me up.

★

I slipped into the car through the half-open door, in wonderment at how my frozen limbs still managed to obey my brain. Montreal in February will give the gulags of Siberia a run for their money.

"*Ki jan w ye, mèt?*" the driver asked me. I had been his passenger before.

"Not bad, not bad."

With the Arctic cold outside, I wouldn't think of answering *m ap boule!* which means "I'm burning," as well as "Things are going great."

In the taxi, an Émeline Michel song was playing, one I didn't know.

"Is that her new record?"

"Who, Émeline? I don't know, it's the radio."

She was a musician we didn't often hear, even on Radio-Canada. But had I forgotten already? In Montreal, Black History Month had been running for the last ten days. For the four most glacial weeks of the year, the contribution of Black communities to Quebec society was celebrated—and no, it wasn't a festival of criminal activity in the northeast sector of the city.

Excuse me, but I have a confession to make. Personally, I'm a little tired of Black History Month in the same way I'm fed up with International Women's Day, World

Book Day, the week to promote the French language or to fight racism. All these causes are legitimate, but the fact of setting aside a day, a week, or a month exasperates me. Call it idealism, but I'm hoping to live in a society that does not need to decree that such and such day will be set aside for such and such cause in order to be sensitized to it.

What's my driver telling me now? I was only half-listening to him, though I suspected he was in the middle of criticizing a panel of intellectuals he had heard debating the crisis in Haiti on the radio the other evening.

Half-measures were not for him. "What really riles me, brother, are all those fashionable leftists with their uptown socialism," he insisted. "Jokers, all of them, if you ask me. It's easy to invent clever analyses and pontificate from your university pulpit, or on a radio show in quiet Montreal. When are they actually going to dare put their boots on the ground and change the way things are back there?"

"Now just a minute," I said, and suggested he adopt a subtler point of view. It was too easy to fall into first-level anti-intellectualism, the kind of demagoguery that has been so destructive in Haiti. He conceded I might have a point, but his anger still burned brightly against the idle Haitian intellectuals of the diaspora.

"While we're at it, I much prefer Charles David to them. At least he went and did something concrete."

Concrete, indeed. That journalist of Haitian origins who had worked for the Montreal daily *La Presse* left his job to join up with the bigwigs of Raoul Cédras' military government, which set off an uproar in the Haitian community.

"And we saw where his actions led him," I retorted. "Now you're just trying to provoke."

"Absolutely not. People wanted to string up David because he took a clear position against the Lavalas family. But didn't history prove he was right?"

Score a point for my driver, I admitted. I had never considered things from that angle.

"Let me tell you something, brother," he went on. "The other evening, I watched your reportage on Haiti, and it was good, very good even."

He was referring to the documentary *Carnet d'un Black en Ayiti*. My filmmaker friend Pierre Bastien had followed me with his camera as I set out to discover the country of my birth, a place I hadn't visited in a quarter century. I accepted my driver's praise, knowing that every compliment hides a criticism.

"Your perspective was interesting, though a little naïve. But it's a start. What do you intend to do now?"

"I don't quite know what you mean."

"I mean for Haiti. What concrete action do you intend to take?"

"Why, wasn't the film enough?" I asked, my turn to provoke.

Judging from my driver's sullen face – no, it obviously was not.

★

I doubt if anyone can forget where he or she was and what he or she was doing on that Tuesday in September 2001, in the morning hours. I was in a taxi, of course—where else?—when the second plane hit the second tower of the World Trade Center. The car was heading from Quebec City's Old Town toward the suburb of Sainte-Foy. I had taken a very early bus from Montreal that morning so I could be at my Quebec City apartment when Videotron arrived to install the cable and high-speed Internet, but first I'd had to make a detour to my office to pick up the network card for my laptop.

It was just past nine when my colleague Antoine, whom I'd crossed paths with during my lightning visit to my office, announced the crash of the first plane. Naturally, twenty minutes later, when I heard the news of the second plane on the radio in the taxi, I thought it was the same information being repeated. A phone call from my friend Jean set me straight.

"Did you hear that?" he laughed cynically over the line. "The Americans are getting a dose of their own medicine."

Jean is one of the few people I can clearly say is more cynical than I am. Before I hung up, I told him that maybe he shouldn't be so jovial. For all we knew, we were standing on the threshold of World War Three.

"Your friend is an odd bird," the driver remarked, a little taken aback.

The man behind the wheel was a woman, this time, and she was taking me to my Quebec City digs. She had obviously heard Jean's enthusiasm over my cell phone. And here I thought that anyone who plied this trade was immunized against all the absurdities of human behaviour, having come face to face with every possible specimen. Apparently, that wasn't the case.

The woman was about to add a few choice words when the radio informed us that a third plane had hit the Pentagon.

"I hope you're not right, but it does seem like the beginnings of the Third World War."

It was time to set aside Jean's cynicism and his easy iconoclasm, and face the facts. Together we were writing a new chapter of our history and entering the twenty-first century head-on.

Like millions of others, I spent the rest of the morning with my eyes glued to the small screen of my television set, as the Twin Towers crumbled like two contemporary replicas of Babel, and with them, a certain idea of world order. Early that afternoon, when the Videotron technician finished installing the cable and put the device through its paces to show us all the channels we could watch now, my girlfriend put on her best faux naïve voice.

"Do you mean we're going to spend fifty dollars every two months to get forty channels that all show the same thing?" she asked dryly.

Her dumb blond imitation was spot-on. The technician stood there, flabbergasted, until he understood she was joking.

I went back to my computer in my downstairs office. I needed to make some final revisions to a short story in the horror genre for my upcoming collection *Le cabinet du docteur K*, a tale of a curse and subsequent revenge which, the evening before, I considered to be terrifying in a completely satisfactory way.

Strange, but the story now seemed laughable.

★

This story goes back a good twenty years, and it served to inspire one of my first short stories.

"Get in, damn it!"

The taxi driver issued that amiable invitation after executing a U-turn so abrupt his tires squealed on the asphalt parking lot I was walking across. He flung the door open, and I got a partial view of the man behind the wheel. Again, he told me to climb into his car.

I was eighteen at the time, and had no scruples and even less awareness of the world.

I accepted his invitation, though I realized that if my father knew what I was doing, he would have a heart attack.

"Where are you going so early in the morning?"

"To the college. Today's registration."

"Good for you. I'll take you there."

The college was a half-hour by foot from my parents' house, and accepting the man's free ride meant I would save a lot of time. I was too carefree to be afraid. All those stories about young men being kidnapped and held in isolated cabins far from civilization—Hollywood could keep them. I had lived most of my life in Jonquière, and the place didn't seem like a likely setting for that sort of scenario. My only reaction was to be intrigued by his disorderly driving, and the way he grasped his cigarette between his greasy, trembling fingers, and that habit he had of constantly turning around to look at the road behind us.

He acted so familiar with me that I figured he was one of my brother Steve's vague acquaintances. He must have mistaken me for him, as happened quite often.

"Goddamn it to hell," he swore between clenched teeth. "I hope those bastards didn't tamper with my brakes."

"Is this the beginning of your shift?"

"No, but pretty soon. At eight!"

Which is why he hadn't flipped on the meter. I wasn't too surprised. After all, I hadn't flagged him down. He'd offered me a ride spontaneously before the official beginning of his shift. With a disgusted look, the man cleared his throat and spat out the window.

"You don't look very happy."

"Why would I be?" He laughed in a sinister fashion, and glanced down quickly at the gas gauge. "I'm running on empty! And I can't gas up. Don't have the money. I'm too fucking poor! A hundred fifty a month, you understand? How can a guy live on that crummy welfare? They're trying to make a fool out of me, and I know it."

The car was moving like a speeding bullet. I asked the driver to slow down. The prospect of dying in an accident in a car driven by a madman didn't really appeal to me. But the guy paid me no mind.

"They're trying to make a fool out of me, I'm telling

you!" he went on, as if we were having a real conversation. "And the worst thing is I can't say a thing about it, otherwise they'll kill me."

I was about to laugh, nervous laughter no doubt, but thought better of it. Maybe change the subject, I decided. But no other subject seemed to interest the driver, completely immersed in his paranoid fantasy.

"The city, the province, the feds—they're all in bed with the maff!"

"The what?" I asked.

"The Mafia, kid! Don't I know it! That's why they've got their eye on me all the time. That's why I can't afford to get to work late. Just the reason they'd use to bump me off, understand?"

He shot me a glance, though I didn't think he was really speaking to me. This was more like a monologue performed by a paranoid guy spitting out his hatred on a society that gave him no chance of fitting in.

And he was driving dangerously fast.

"Yeah, kid, I know way too much for my own good. That's why they want to get rid of me. I bet you think I'm crazy, right?"

I didn't answer, and it didn't matter. He wasn't looking for an answer.

"All this shit wouldn't have happened if I would have stayed in school," he said, in a philosophical mood suddenly. "Do your college, kid, finish it. Study hard and be smarter than anyone else so they can't fuck you over the way they fucked me over. Study, and tell your friends to be like you. It's too late for me and guys like me. Our days are numbered. The first chance they think they can get away with it, they'll have my ass!"

Those were the final words he spoke. We reached the college and he pulled over. I asked him if I owed him anything, but he waved his hand in my face. He had been able to confide in a sympathetic and attentive person, and that was payment enough.

I got out of the car and wished him well. As I walked toward the main student entrance, I remembered thinking that I had an interesting subject for a short story: a paranoid driver entrusts his fear of being murdered as part of a master plot to a perfect stranger who turns out to be his killer. I even decided I'd call the story "Get in, damn it!"

I ended up publishing a fictionalized version of this anecdote in my collection *Treize pas vers l'inconnu*, but with the title "Un Drôle de Pistolet," suggested by the publisher Robert Soulières.

As for the guy behind the wheel, I never saw him again. Sometimes I wonder whether "they" ended up knocking him off, as he was afraid they would.

★

The least you could say is the old Black man with the run-down look was honest.

"You're going to have to show me the way, sir. I don't know this area at all," he confessed when I got in his car.

Fine with me. I appreciated his sincerity, which disproved that shop-worn prejudice according to which not only do most Haitian taximen have no idea of the geography of the city, they have no sense of direction either. And they're dishonest and won't think twice about taking the long way rather than admit they don't know where a certain place is. With his confession, the old man became sympathetic. But how old could he be? I would say sixty, easily, maybe seventy, but something in his voice told me he could be even older.

Too bad my friendly feeling was not reciprocated. As soon as we took our spot on the back seat, I felt him tense up, as if we weren't welcome in his vehicle. The two of us were loaded down like mules, carrying aluminum containers, the buffet I'd prepared for a dinner with friends.

With the excuse of helping me with the preparations, my colleague, a born-and-raised Quebec woman, had spent the afternoon at my place in hopes of learning how to cook the traditional Haitian dishes: red beans and rice, *griyo*—marinated, fried pork—a dish of *akra lanmoru*—

fritters made of salt cod and manioc flour—shrimp in an eggplant sauce, fried plantains, the usual line-up. I'm not as skillful a cook as my mother was, or even my father, but I'm no slouch in the kitchen.

I wasn't sure my friend would retain my cooking lessons, but we had a great time—and the party hadn't even started.

My directions for how to get to our destination were as clear as could be, so I figured we would arrive safe and sound before the dishes had time to cool down. The Haitian community radio station was playing an old version of a song that was even older, part of the popular repertory. I knew the music. Suddenly, like the aroma of a spicy broth, the past returned: Sunday afternoons with my family in Jonquière. Between lunch and an episode of the old Japanese sci-fi TV series *Ultraman* that came on early in the evening, my mother Lady I. would play her records, jazz or some variety thereof, or maybe French popular songs, or classical or Haitian music. Between Nat King Cole and the Orchestre Septentrional, the choice would depend on the mood of the lady of the house.

My friend was something of a jazz singer, and she was quick to pick up on the music.

"Who's that singing?" she asked.

"I think it's Toto Bissainthe… unless it's Martha Jean-Claude. I'm not sure. I haven't heard that piece in years."

In the rear-view mirror, I saw the driver's eyes open wide.

"Toto Bissainthe, yes," he confirmed. Then he added,

"Ho, m pa ta janm kwè yon blan tankou ou menm ta konnen chante sa a."

One more guy who had quickly filed me away in the category of fake Haitians, completely acculturated. "I would have never thought a White like you would know these songs." If only one day we could live without having to parade around, holding a flag.

"Of course I know those songs," I answered him in Creole. "It's the music of my childhood."

In the lowering light of early evening, his smile, pure white, lit up his dark face like a crescent moon in an inky sky.

"So, you're Haitian," the old man replied. "Well, now I understand the aroma from those packages you have."

I ran through the menu with the intent of making him salivate.

"Se ou menm ki fè tout manje sa a poukont ou."

"Mwen menm ki fè'l menm, " I answered with no small amount of pride. Of course I cooked it all myself!

My friend gave me a penetrating look. My Quebec friends are always astonished to hear me speak Creole. And my Haitian friends are indulgent enough not to point out the mistakes I inevitably make in their language.

The old man put up the volume for the next song. *"Ayiti cheri, pi bon peyi passe ou nan pwen …."* I couldn't help feeling sadness in my heart. My mother tried to ease her dying husband's pain with that song in the cancer ward of the Jonquière hospital.

"Haiti, there is no better country than you …." The

first line of the refrain of Dr. Othello Bayard's famous *Haïti chérie*, a song also known as *Souvenirs d'Haïti*. There is not a better lament an exile might sing.

Suddenly the old driver wanted to talk. He was interested in us: what we did for a living, the nature of our relationship (no, we weren't a couple!), what kind of party we were going to…

A shame we were already reaching our destination. But we wouldn't leave him empty-handed. Wrapped up in a napkin, my friend and I left him a little ration of *griyo*, a few *akras*, and two pieces of fried plantain to go with the tip.

★

"The corner of Sainte-Catherine and Saint-Urbain, please. Drop me off by the Radio-Canada tent."

"That's funny, it's not Sunday noon…"

That was the driver's way of telling me he recognized me, and that he sometimes tuned in to the book show on the radio I host for Sunday brunch. Though currently he was listening to one of those religious programs on Haitian radio, the sort of diet I try to avoid.

"Nothing to do with *Bouquinville* today. Besides, the show takes the summer off," I explained to him. "And I won't be back on the air come autumn. I've been hosting a jazz show since the middle of June. It runs till the end of August."

"Then what will happen?"

His concern, with its hint of paternalism, touched me. I imagined he had children my age who were experiencing the precarious nature of the job market, typical of our times. But he didn't need worry about me. Something would always turn up.

"Time will tell," I said to him.

The downtown traffic was moving reasonably well. I shouldn't be any later than normal.

"I didn't know you were a jazz expert," the driver launched in.

"Expert—that's not a claim I'd make. Let's just say I'm pretty good for an amateur."

"What are we going to hear on your show?"

"The usual, classics from the past and present… Louis Armstrong and Billie Holiday, Ella Fitzgerald and Miles Davis, plus some contemporary musicians I like."

"Are you going to play Haitian jazz?"

The inevitable question, which I was waiting for.

"I intend to play the Haitian artists I think people should hear. I'm thinking of Azor, Edy Brisseaux, Éval Manigat, Eddy Prophète, Beethova Obas for certain of his pieces. And then there's a new guy, a saxophonist by the name of Buyu Ambroise who just put out a record."

"What about Tabou Combo? And Coupé Cloué? And Boukman Experyans?"

"I don't think they could be considered jazz in the proper sense—"

"How can you say that?"

Here was an old misunderstanding that just wouldn't go away. It resulted from the confusion in the meaning that Creole-speakers gave the word "jazz," and the meaning most other people had in mind. The driver and I agreed to pursue our scholarly discussions about musical terminology another time. Especially since the crew was waiting for me on the esplanade of Place des Arts, where our live show would be broadcast from.

"*Kenbe, frèr. Ma va koute w aswè a,*" he promised as he gave me my change.

In that case, the driver wouldn't be disappointed. I had

asked my friend Anthony Rozankovic, who was taking care of the music for the show, to make sure and play *Choucoune*.

I had a family connection, albeit distant, to that famous popular song composed in 1883 by the Haitian Louisiana pianist Michel Mauléart Monton, based on the poem "Frè P'tit Pierre" by the Cap-Haïtien poet Oswald Durand—one of my forebears on my mother's side. Wrongly attributed to Irving Burgie, who simply adapted the piece into English and gave it the title *Yellowbird*, the song had international success in the 1950s thanks to Harry Belafonte's version of it.

★

His cell phone conversation absorbed him so completely I wasn't sure whether he knew I had gotten into his car. Ah, he had noticed: he replaced the phone in the holder and started the engine in hands-free mode.

"*Se bò lakay ou wap fè, konpè?*" he asked me over his shoulder.

I nodded. Yes, I was going to my house. He knew the way; we had often driven together. The taxi started up Saint-Hubert, heading north.

"*Ou fout tombe sou tèt ou?*" he burst out.

Haitian fathers are all alike. This one could have been my father Mèt Mo bawling out my brother Reynald, the black sheep of the family.

As he carried on his tumultuous conversation with a female voice on the other end of the line—his daughter, I was presuming—I used the break in the action—for me, not for him—to unwrap the records I had bought. I can't help it, I'm like a kid at Christmas, I love opening CDs and reading the liner notes until I can finally slip the record into the machine. I was so concentrated on my reading material that I didn't realize the taxi had turned the wrong way on Saint-Joseph.

I figured I had the right to break into his conversation and point out his mistake. He was so embarrassed he put a rapid end to his family conflict.

"*Bon, dakò. Na pale pita, m di'w,*" he said, and hung up the phone.

Then, turning around, he asked, "You don't live on Cartier anymore?"

"No, I moved in July. Sorry, I should have told you."

"No need! I should have checked the address."

And since there were no police in sight, my driver executed an illegal turn at the next corner and headed west, toward my new residence.

"You look preoccupied," I told him. "Troubles, maybe?"

"*Tèt chaje, mèt, tèt chaje!* My daughter and her unreasonable demands. She gives me headaches! Lately, ever since she started going out with that *vagabond*, she's changed. She doesn't come home when she's supposed to, she goes out and doesn't say where she is, and she had a ring put in her nose. Worse, she talks to her mother in a tone that's completely unacceptable, and acts high and mighty when we tell her she has to come home at night. Just now, she was trying to tell me it's normal for her boyfriend to sleep over at the house. Can you imagine—under my roof!"

"How old is your daughter?"

"Fifteen, I'm telling you. Only fifteen!"

I sympathized with the driver. I wasn't exactly a *vagabond*—a ne'er-do-well—but neither was I the best-behaved teenager in my day. My mother could have attested to that. My run-ins with Mèt Mo weren't that frequent, but they could heat up in a hurry. And I was lucky: I was a boy. With time, I came to understand the gap between the rules of the traditional Haitian upbringing, and those that govern families in Quebec. How I wished I had the latter's free and easy ways in my house! Our Haitian parents apparently had no idea how difficult it was for their children to accept the constraints they imposed on them, while their home-grown Quebec friends the same age lived in a totally permissive atmosphere—or so it seemed to us.

"In any case, raising a daughter—I wouldn't wish it on anyone, starting with you."

"Too late."

"Ou gen pitit?" he said, surprised. *"Yon fiy?"*

I nodded. Not only did I have children, but one of them was a girl. I wasn't claiming to be the perfect father, but I tried my best. To cheer up the driver, I decided to share a little story with him.

"You know as well as I do how irritating their endless demands can be. One day, a couple of years ago, I was so exasperated I told my daughter, enough is enough, I explained how it works to you, and it's up to you to obey without fussing or fighting, because I'm your father and I make the rules here, and as long as you live in my house you will have to accept that. I really didn't want to go back to those old ways of setting myself up as the authority, the way my own father did, because I hated that argument when he used to trot it out. But I was fed up. And you know what she told me?"

I had piqued the driver's curiosity. He waited for what

would come next.

"My daughter Laura said, Well, then, I'll go find my-self an apartment. The only problem was she was two-and-a-half years old."

"Two-and-a-half?"

The driver burst out in rich, hearty laughter.

"*Ho, pitit sa a pa nan jwèt, kompè! W antrave, mon chè.* Your troubles are only just beginning. You've got your-self a live wire!"

★

I sought refuge from the wind and snow in the first cab that showed up.

"Radio-Canada, please," I said to the driver. Then I collapsed onto the back seat.

"You're at the end of your rope from what I can see," he declared. When I remarked on his French accent, he wasted no time pointing out he was from Brittany, which was not quite the same thing as France. "What's going on?"

What's going on? I wondered whether he was joking.

I felt as if I'd accidentally wandered into an episode of one of those science-fiction TV series I have always appreciated. All that was missing was Rod Serling, standing to one side of the action and commenting in a dead-pan soliloquy on the extraordinary chain of unexpected events. Since the previous evening, when I temporarily turned my attention away from my suitcases to meet my friend Athésia, who happened to be returning from Haiti, I had literally been projected into the *Twilight Zone*. First, my friend Christophe informed me about the disaster and asked me if I still intended to travel to Port-au-Prince on the plane that was to leave Montreal at dawn on January 13. Then I learned from Delta Airlines that the flight was cancelled. Having spent most of the evening with friends who had wanted to have dinner with me before my return to my native land, I was awoken at dawn by a researcher from Radio-Canada current events. She was triumphant: she had managed to get hold of me on my cell phone.

"That's it, I've made contact!" she called to her colleagues from the morning show.

"What's all the excitement about? I'm in Montreal."

Though I didn't know it, the all-news, down-market TV channel LCN, as well-informed as usual, had launched the rumour the previous evening that "nothing has been heard from the writer Stanley Péan who, along with his colleague Dany Laferrière, is currently in Port-au-Prince to take part in a literary festival."

I declined the researcher's invitation to comment on the earthquake, just as I refused interviews with the print media. After all, I didn't know anything more than anyone else in Canada. I was just as dependent on news from Haiti as the people here who wanted to record my impressions for broadcast. But then, a few hours later, I ended up going back on my initial position, and agreed to go on air with my friend Luck Mervil on Simon Durivage's show on RDI, the Radio-Canada news channel, if only to put a stop to the persistent rumour according to which I was, like Dany, or worse, like poor Georges Anglade, the writer, trapped in the rubble of Port-au-Prince. I spoke live of the distress I shared with so many members of the Haitian diaspora in Montreal, and with their Quebec sympathizers—but would venture no further than that. On the TV set, Luck Mervil recruited me to help out the CECI (the

Centre d'études et de coopération internationale) that had begun organizing a program to accept donations of goods that would be useful on the ground where the NGO was well established.

All that afternoon of January 13, 2010, surrounded by the constant racket of ringing telephones, shoulder to shoulder with volunteers who had graciously accepted to devote their time to the CECI to help the Haitians hit with one more in the endless chain of disasters they clearly did not need, I answered questions from TV and radio journalists who were trying to reach me. In my modest way I helped lessen the panic and anxiety, and I did my best to make myself useful, even from this distance. I also agreed to write a piece for the daily paper *Le Devoir* for the next day. My article spoke of my refusal to surrender to cynicism and despair, and I wanted to share that sentiment with my compatriots back home and those living here. Then I gathered my things and went to join other colleagues shoe-horned into the basement of a church that had been converted into a community centre where the evening network news would be broadcast that evening.

So you can imagine that I was more than taken aback by the ignorance of the driver who was taking me to the Radio-Canada building, where I would participate in a special show about the events hosted by media personality Franco Nuovo. Was the driver living in a parallel universe?

To the music of radio station Rock Détente ("Relaxed Rock") that was playing in his car, I gave him a quick overview: the force of the initial tremor, the deadly after-shocks, the images of the destruction that had been running on all the media since the day before, the number of casualties that were clearly higher than the first estimates, the impossibility of reaching family or friends in the country, and the tragic death of my colleague Georges Anglade and his wife Mireille who were in the country as part of the same literary festival called "Étonnants voyageurs."

How did my driver from Brittany explain away his unawareness of the human tragedy being played out in the former "Pearl of the Antilles?" He said he didn't listen much to the news because it was too depressing.

A few days later, my son Philippe, not yet five years old, came up with this description that was clever, yes, but that chilled my blood all the same. He was tired of all those grown-ups around him who were so involved and so frenetic about a tragedy they could do nothing about.

"You know, Papa," Philippe told me, "on Teletoon they only play cartoons, and a little advertising, and they never talk about earthquakes."

I suppose my taxi driver from Brittany would have agreed with my little boy.

But such a lack of awareness—how is it possible?

★

The day after the earthquake in Haiti, the organizers of the Étonnants voyageurs literary festival suggested that the writers who had been invited to Port-au-Prince, and who could obviously not travel there now, should join the Saint-Malo edition of the event. The activities that were to have taken place on my island would now be moved to the small, picturesque port city in Brittany—that region again!

After the weekend of discussions and public events, along with the rest of my colleagues, I took the special Saint-Malo to Paris train chartered by the event. I was riding with my friend Michel Vézina in an economy-class car.

In the restaurant car, we were shocked to see what happened to the African-American bluesman Ladell McLin, who had politely asked the people in line ahead of him if they wouldn't mind letting him go to the front and order something quickly for his son whose health was fragile. The waiter refused rudely, and even challenged the American musician's right to be on board.

"He's wearing a Festival badge," a woman at the counter pointed out.

"That means nothing, Ma'am. We don't know where he found it. There are any number of passengers who slip onto these trains even if they don't have the right to be here."

The little genius couldn't even run his electronic payment device, but he knew enough to make a judgement like that? Racial profiling was running wild in France, a leftover from the Sarkozy era, according to Michel Vézina, whose threshold of tolerance for racism and other human stupidities stood at just about zero. One more comment from the waiter and Vézina, who is built like a brick you-know-what, and is even bigger than I am, would have communicated his point of view to him with a right cross. After informing the arrogant waiter that McLin was one of the Festival guests, which was a complete waste of my saliva, I defused the situation by ordering something to eat for his son and him as soon as I reached the counter.

Three hours later, we pulled into Montparnasse station in Paris, and since we were heading in different directions, Vézina and I bid each other farewell at the taxi stand, and made a solemn promise to get together as soon as possible back in Montreal. The lady behind the wheel of my cab—Italian or Spanish, I couldn't identify her accent, I must have been too tired—asked me where I was from, and where I was going. I answered with few words, not much in the mood for a chat. We were moving up the one-way approach next to the station when she started honking at a car backing up the wrong way in our direction, apparently with a view to finding a place to park.

"What the hell is he doing?" my driver shouted, but there was no way to avoid the collision.

The "he" behind the wheel of the other car turned out to be a "she," and a pretty one. She popped out of her cab to inspect the damage.

"I didn't do that," she stated, less in denial, and more in disbelief.

But the nuance escaped my driver who was all aflame with outrage, demanding an apology, a joint report, and, above all else, an admission of guilt from the other driver. There I was in Paris, the world capital of useless, picturesque shouting matches. The tone quickly headed for the gutter, and the two women each tried to recruit me as their witness.

"Monsieur, you can see she's a crazy hysteric," said the driver at fault, who was ready to admit her mistake as long as she could come to a reasonable agreement with my driver.

"Me, crazy? I'm hysterical? But Monsieur, you saw her back down this one-way lane the wrong way as if it belonged to her, and meanwhile, I'm leaning on the horn to keep her from crashing into me!"

It was too late to reason. These two women weren't born to get along, and besides, neither had a blank joint report form in her glove compartment. My driver flagged down a few of her colleagues who were trying to use the lane that we were half-blocking, but unfortunately they couldn't help her. And I was prisoner of a quarrel that didn't concern me, but too exhausted to try to escape it. My hotel was close by, fifteen minutes on foot at most, but I had opted for a taxi because I didn't feel strong enough to walk there with my burden of heavy suitcases.

While the Sunday cab driver got on her cell phone to call her husband whom she was supposed to meet, my taxiwoman, out of patience, decided to call the police. I didn't want to question her judgement, but in my experience, calling the cops to settle a cat-fight has never settled anything for anyone, no matter where you are in the world. The police van showed up a few minutes later, remarkably quickly, just as the guilty driver's husband made an appearance. He and I were quickly relegated to the status of second-rate witnesses by the hefty men in uniform. Hefty men, and hefty numbers: there were five of them. Five officers dispatched for a simple fender bender between two cabs, with no victim outside of the car's martyred bumper? Will wonders never cease? This was France under law-and-order President Sarkozy in all its splendour, and I was exasperated when I pictured my friend Vézina who must have been sleeping like a baby in his hotel room by now, lucky guy! Police state or not, I was ordered to stay on the back seat until the issue was resolved.

The affair took a more complicated turn when the police demanded that the guilty party take a breathalyzer test, which provided damning evidence.

"But I only had one glass of bubbly at the *apéro*, just one, I swear," protested the young woman, caught red-handed.

My taxiwoman was jubilant; at last she had irrefutable proof of her adversary's gross negligence. The policemen's verdict came down: everyone off to the station where the presumed guilty driver would undergo a more rigorous test to see exactly what manner of accusation would be levelled against her.

"At least you can let me drop my customer at his hotel on the way there," my driver appealed to the officers.

It was about time! On the other hand, the entire drama had become so absurd that I was almost sorry that the officer in charge of the operation consented to grant me my leave. Was it my professional instincts, or maybe just to kill time, but I started building the outline of a crime story I could base on this banal event. What if, as in Francis Weber's *L'Emmerdeur*, I were a hired killer caught against my will in a minor accident that threatened to cancel the contract I had to execute in the next thirty minutes...

I would never find out how this soap opera ended, because the lady driver with the Latin temperament dropped me off at my hotel, forty-five minutes behind schedule.

"Don't bother, sir," she said, waving off my money for the fare. "I told you I'd drive you free of charge to thank you for your patience."

I slid my euros back into my pocket, stepped out of the car, and retrieved my bags from the trunk. I was weary, but still a shade disappointed at having to depend solely on my imagination to plot out the conclusion of this urban adventure.

★

The sentence fell with the finality of a guillotine.

"The man is a scoundrel," decreed Monsieur Alex, the manager of my Paris hotel, a sympathetic Kabyle who maintained he had met Albert Camus (there are no accidents in life!), and who adopted me the first day I set foot in his establishment.

The scoundrel in question was Ben, the Arab taxi driver who had brought me from my supper with my old friend Aline at the Cour St-Émilion to my rendezvous with Paula at the Odéon subway last evening, and who had promised to pick me up at my hotel at exactly eight forty-five this morning to take me to the airport for a flight to Oslo.

The scoundrel never did show up, and he didn't bother answering when I called his cell phone. The result: I waited nearly an hour for another car that Monsieur Alex managed to get a hold of from another company—that's Paris for you. Maybe because I am blessed by those gods I don't believe in, the new driver, a Haitian by the name of Lubin, was able to bypass all the bottlenecks the French capital is famous for.

On the way to my destination, we made our act of recognition, so to speak, the way Haitians always end up recognizing each other no matter where they meet on this planet. When we did, our conversation naturally switched from the language of Molière to that of Languichatte, though I am hardly a master of Creole, it goes without saying, but no matter. Lubin had never heard of me as a writer and even less as a radio host, but he had a friend who was also his business partner who lived in Montreal, and who had spoken kindly of me. He asked about my life and career in Canada, and described his own journey from his teenage years in Haiti, the studies he dropped too soon and against his will, his years managing a factory, his arrival in France, and the endless hours he spent behind the wheel of his taxi to feed his rather large family.

We talked Haitian history and politics, of course. We talked disasters, natural and other, as well as the relationship between history, politics, and all the other catastrophes of our time. *Nap bay lodyans, kòmanman.*

"You know, no matter how many years I've spent in this White country, and even if I've raised my children here, no one will ever convince me that Haiti isn't my home," he declared.

Lubin and his partner Quesner had a project: they wanted to open a resort hotel in the Dominican Republic.

"You know, we wanted to open it in our country, but with the political uncertainty in Haiti…"

We talked on, and the conversation was so absorbing that I forgot I was in a hurry. I didn't even realize my fellow countryman had succeeded in driving me from the Latin Quarter to Terminal 2F in forty minutes flat, just one-half hour before take-off. Time would be tight, but

I would be able to check in, drop off my bag, go through security, and run full-speed to the gate five minutes before it closed.

As he handed me my bags, Lubin promised to drive me to the airport the following Sunday, the day after my return from Norway, when I would be flying back to Canada. As well, would I mind being the messenger and bringing a package back for his Montreal associate?

I took Lubin seriously. I called him the evening I came back from Norway to make sure he would be in front of my hotel the next day to take me to the airport. My compatriot was a man of his word. Not just on time but early, he walked into the lobby and helped me carry my heavy bags to his minivan. He was sorry, but he hadn't had time to finalize the information he was supposed to give me to transfer to his Montreal partner, but no harm done.

The traffic was a lot easier than the other morning, and I would have several hours to spare before the plane departed. As we talked, we returned to the themes we had explored the first time—a kind of deepening of the field, you might say.

He drove, and we conversed like a couple of brothers who had been separated by a long absence, and who were together at last. We reinvented Haiti and the world at large, both of which definitely needed our help.

I looked out the window and thought, I like this new brother. He's a good man.

"*Pa bliye, non,*" Lubin said as he handed me my bags in front of the terminal. "You have to call Quesner when you get to Montreal. Just to give him my regards."

And I completely forgot to do it... until I wrote these lines!

I reached for the telephone to call him.

★

"Home, sir?"

The question was both rhetorical and somewhat amusing. It conjured up those films in which a driver in livery asks the question he knows the answer to, as the rich businessman slumps onto the backseat of the limousine, exhausted after a tumultuous meeting of the board of directors.

Since June of 2009, my Montreal evenings have followed the exact same pattern. From Monday to Thursday, I leave the studio shortly after eight in the evening and climb into the first taxi at the head of the line at the Radio-Canada / CBC building, then head for my apartment. The trip takes fifteen minutes or so, often with the same drivers who, with the passage of time, do not have to ask my address. If we believe Martha, the main character in Albert Camus' play *The Misunderstanding*, habit sets in with the second time.

For a number of months, it's true, my final destination temporarily changed, not because I had moved as one of "my" drivers presumed, but thanks to a passionate love affair that had me spending my evenings and nights in the condo that my *chérie* had bought in the east end. The ride there included a stop I was only too happy to make: the liquor store to buy a bottle of chilled Nicolas Feuillate.

My lover and I enjoyed the tiny bubbles, and though at times she thought I was prone to excess, she never turned down one more flute of champagne.

Les histoires d'amour finissent mal en général, so sings Catherine Ringer of the French pop group Les Rita Mitsouko. For those who have no notion of that language, love affairs usually end up tanking. I have heard that refrain too often in my life, and unfortunately this affair was clearly not going to be an exception to the rule. Not enough trust on either side, no doubt. Despite my concerted efforts, I was never able to dissipate my lover's suspicions about my infidelity, and she turned suspicions into unshakable conviction with all the weight that implies. In the long run, even the bottles of champagne and other occasional marks of affection took on, in her eyes, the appearance of devastating elements of proof. "The only reason you're so generous," she would accuse me one day, just before the end, "is to try and divert my attention from your duplicitous nature!" Well, she might not have said it in those exact terms, but her charge did have that hurtful sort of theatricality.

We were still several months from the end, that winter evening, but the atmosphere was far from smooth. Had I called her from the taxi to announce I would soon be there? Probably. What else would account for the driver's open-hearted concern about the signs of tumult in my love life?

"Sak pase, mèt? Sanble madanm ou ap baw tèt chaje?"

And what is going on, am I preoccupied with troubles with a certain lady?

As cordial as my relations are with a number of taxi-men in whose cars I travel on a daily basis, I have never been the kind to open up to them and spontaneously confide in strangers. Who knows why, this time I turned away from my usual prudery and told him about the cause of my headaches, the *tèt chaje*, or loaded head, as they say in Creole.

The driver's reaction and the advice that followed made me smile. Could I agree with him without giving the impression that I was validating atavisms, clichés, and well-worn ideas? Even today, many Haitian men, what-ever their generation, display outdated machismo in their love affairs. The driver tried to explain that what matters is not whether or not I see other women, but that I reas-sure my darling as to her special status, her legitimacy. Just like her, he understood nothing. And like her, he could not accept the fact that I would have a relationship that was fully exclusive.

★★★

The rest, as I came to understand with the passage of time, was sadly ordinary. *Les histoires d'amour finissent mal en général*, and the general will always win out over what we naively assume will be particular. My sweetheart broke off with me a third time at summer's end, when we returned from a trip to France I had invited her on, "to try and divert her attention from my duplicitous nature," as she put it.

With a broken heart, I trudged through my routine on the radio, evening after evening. Because that's life, and life continues despite everything, and the pain of lost love is not fatal.

A few weeks later, when I climbed into his car, the same Haitian driver assumed, quite naturally, that he should head east, toward the condo where I was no longer welcome.

"No," I told him. "My house."

I gave him the address in case he had forgotten it. In the rear-view mirror, I caught his expression, a combination of surprise and incredulity.

But he didn't ask any questions. And I was glad of that.

★

"Ah, M'sieu Péan, it's been a while!" he exclaimed as I settled onto the back seat of the vehicle.

I looked in the rear-view mirror to see who he could be. The part of his face I could make out beneath the shadow of his fedora was vaguely familiar, but not enough to identify him.

"You don't recognize me? We spent a whole evening driving through Montreal with your colleague from Radio-Canada, Madame Charbonneau, I believe her name was."

Ah, yes, he pronounced the magic words, and like the delicate Monsieur Proust biting into his *madeleine*, I was inundated with a wave of memories. More than a dozen years had elapsed since the evening in question spent recording a sequence of *Ayiti P.Q.*, Dominique Charbonneau's radio documentary, a sort of urban travelogue about the cultural impact of Montreal's Haitian community on the city where most of its members had decided to settle.

The driver insisted on refreshing my memory; he introduced formally himself. Louis L. Mêmeil, alias the Taximan Troubadour. Of course I remembered him. I even had a copy of his album somewhere in my disorderly record collection: *Célébrez Québec avec Louis L. Mêmeil, Taximan Troubadour.*

A teacher in Haiti, like a good number of compatriots, he fled into exile to escape the dictatorship. He lived in Paris, trying his luck as a crooner, then moved to the United States. He came to Montreal on vacation, was charmed by the city, and decided to settle there. He worked in real estate without much luck, and then returned to Haiti and opened a series of restaurants.

After another in the long parade of coups d'état that marked the history of Haitian politics in the post-dictatorship era, he headed for Montreal again. A quarter-century later, he became a piece of contemporary folklore. "I took a class to learn to be a taxi driver and I bought a licence. I love the job. Every day, I meet different people who tell me their story, and talk about their daily lives, and discuss what's happening in the world. Often I am their guide to the city, I tell them things about my life too. I have found my happiness with these people, in their smile." Or so says the page dedicated to the Taximan Troubadour on the official site of the City of Montreal.

We were on boulevard Saint-Joseph, heading east. Mê-meil asked after Dominique Charbonneau, since he had appreciated her company for the brief time they worked together. I told him she had left Radio-Canada, and we hadn't stayed in touch. Our conversation moved along, with anecdotes about life in Quebec, memories of Haiti, and no end of joking.

As he always did, he slipped his CD into the player and began singing along to his own recording. I recognized the song, "Mama de Mêmeil" that he once sang in a bar for Mother's Day, invited on stage by a singer he knew. The piece is solemn, a bolero tune, and speaks of his late mother and the sacrifices she made to provide her children with a better life. According to the legend recorded on the City's page about Mêmeil, the people who had gathered in the bar appreciated the song so deeply they demanded an encore immediately. The day after his triumph, the Taximan Troubadour entered a studio and recorded his album.

Louis L. Mêmeil freely admits he has no ambitions about a career on stage, in the spotlight. Breaking into that world is not for everyone. Besides, the Taximan Troubadour reports he has found happiness already.

I told him about the new edition of my book *Taximan*, and how I intend to make his story part of it. He recommended I do a little research on YouTube, where there are several short videos about him. One of these clips made by director Jacques Thivierge (whose work regularly screens on *Second Regard* and *Le Point*, and who has sketched the portraits of a number of artists for the ARTV channel), and simply called *Louis L. Mêmeil, Taximan Troubadour*, ends with these words that perfectly sum up Mêmeil's personal philosophy: "I don't sell happiness. Happiness is there before us. It's simply there, like the song says. Happiness is in your heart. Don't look any further. It's inside you. And that's the truth!"

★

"If I understand correctly, your new book features a number of cab drivers," said this particular driver, with whom I had not travelled in a while.

"That's it, exactly."

"That's odd, because from my point of view, I get all sorts of strange specimens riding in my car."

I am sure that's the case. A few years back, I read *Un taxi la nuit* (Septentrion, 2007), a collection of pieces written by Pierre-Léon Lalonde, who was equipped with a literature degree but had been driving a cab since the early 1990s. In the book, he portrayed his most picturesque passengers and told the tale of his most unusual fares. Once, with random chance on my side, I took a ride in the cab driven by the taximan writer, which gave us the opportunity to discuss our respective books whose points of view were both opposite and complementary.

That afternoon, my driver was adamant about the often unhealthy character of the nocturnal animals who appeared when the bars and nightclubs closed; for that reason he worked days only. "You have no idea, Monsieur Péan! You get guys who are completely drunk, and you have to make them repeat their address three times because their diction is so sloppy, and when you reach their destination they start yelling at you because they claim you didn't take them to the right place. Not to mention the young people whose minds are so addled by drugs they're willing to jump out of the car at a red light to avoid paying you. And then there are those shifty characters who pull a knife on you in hopes of getting their hands on the few banknotes you have. And what about those shameless, passionate couples who are an inch away from total intimacy on the backseat without a thought for the driver looking at them in the mirror? And while we're at it, I've had my share of penniless seducers who want to pay for their fare with their bodies. I've seen every possible human act, I swear on Jesus and His Mother!"

I was not about to forget this particular story. "Once my fare was a magnificent young woman, really very sexy, and provocatively dressed, at the limit of being vulgar. She gave me the address where she was going, then added that she needed to make a stop along the way, only a minute, no more, to get something at a friend's house. It was late, I was exhausted, I'd been behind the wheel for more than seven hours. I stopped in front of the apartment building where her friend supposedly lived, and she went inside. I waited. And waited. I waited fifteen minutes until I understood I'd been swindled, she must have gone out the back door, and that she had never intended to pay me."

★

That story reminded me of another that a different Haitian driver told me a few days later, as we travelled along the wide street that runs past Lafontaine Park. He was furious at having been cut off, though he knew it would happen, by a distracted driver in the lane for cars turning left on Rachel instead of continuing on rue de la Roche. My driver started honking and swearing in Creole. I couldn't help it: I spared a fond thought for my late father who was so quick to anger at the wheel.

"I'm telling you, Monsieur Péan, this job is no joke! Imagine, this very morning, something untoward happened to me not far from here. Dispatch sent me to pick up two people at a luxury hotel downtown, an older gentleman who spoke English and a woman quite a bit younger than him, very pretty, and who didn't seem to be his wife, if you know what I mean… I turned over the meter and went east along Sherbrooke toward Amherst, as they told me to. In the back, the older gentleman was confirming a meeting on his phone, and trying to agree with the other party on the price of a certain transaction, illicit by the sound of it."

Immediately, sensing that the plot was about to thicken, the crime-story fan in me was captivated. I couldn't help but remember a rather so-so thriller by Michael

Mann, *Collateral*, in which Vincent, a hired gun played by Tom Cruise, press-gangs a cab driver named Max (Jamie Fox) and his car to take him to the addresses of his next victims.

My driver continued. "When I reached Sherbrooke and Amherst, I parked the way they asked me to. In my mirror, I saw the man give the woman a handful of twenty-dollar bills. He whispered his instructions to her. The girl got out of the car and walked over to one parked sideways, next to mine. She climbed in. The man watched her like a hawk—a worried hawk. I looked away from the mirror, I was not very happy to be tied up in this risky business, even indirectly. I turned on the radio and picked up my newspaper. I didn't need to look at him: I could feel his impatience. He started swearing. 'Shit, they're leaving!' He was right. The other car headed east on Sherbrooke with the girl inside. 'Shit, shit, shit!' That swear word was his litany. 'The bitch took my cash! Quick, don't let them get away!'"

"And what did you do?"

"What do you think I did? The light had turned red, and my customer was banging away on the headrest of the seat and shouting, 'Follow them, for Chrissake!' But I didn't do any such thing. I waited for him to calm down a little, then told him I wasn't going to follow that car, he could always get out of mine and hail another cab in the street, he could not pay me, I was happy to drive him this far for free but I wasn't going to get involved in his business, I loved life too much."

"What did he say?"

"Thank God, he relaxed a little, then leaned back on the seat, and gave a great sigh. Then, discouraged, but not too much, he asked me to drive him back to his hotel. I never knew who he was, and what the nature of the aborted transaction was. I left him exactly where I had picked him up not long before. He paid, but didn't leave me a tip. Needless to say, I didn't insist."

★

"M'sieur Péan, you are a writer, a journalist, an intellectual…"

This preface to the question, which I am dreading, by the way, makes it possible for me to anticipate what will come next word for word, or almost. Mind you, this driver and I have developed a companionship thanks to our many trips across Montreal. One of the first times I was his passenger, he completely lost his way, confusing the rue Marconi where my meeting was with a wholly different street in the city's east end. I was busy reading my emails on my phone and was not paying attention to where we were going. Too late, I noticed the landscape was all wrong. The driver was embarrassed and refused to take my money, but I wouldn't hear of it.

Since that time, I have always enjoyed the best possible service with him. Sometimes, we even stock up on our wine and spirits together – with the meter snoozing, of course. And our rides are always spiced up by discussions on any number of subjects that concern both of us, be they social, political, or cultural.

Not long ago, he described all the details surrounding the mess involved in his brother's succession back home, which forced him to spend a month in the country to liquidate the late gentleman's property as he moved through the complications generated by Haitian bureaucracy, worthy of a Franz Kafka novel, with corruption added on top. In return, I told him of the two-week vacation I had gone on with my teenage daughter Laura who, ever since she was a child, had dreamed of discovering the island where half her family comes from. As the winter of 2017 settled in, with a single voice and a heavy heart, he and I mourned the passing of Manno Charlemagne, the singer-songwriter-composer and political activist the foreign press had dubbed "the Haitian Bob Dylan," though the comparison does not quite hold up.

Along the route of our conversations, my driver evaluated the progress of my spoken Creole, using his native kindness and sense of humour. My language was less bookish, he said, and more natural, more fluid over time.

Lately, our conversations have had a new stimulus: Donald Trump's famous statement associating El Salvador, the majority of African nations, and our beloved Haiti with primitive latrines – "shithole countries," as he put it – inhabited by people less worthy of the right to immigrate to the United States than a Norwegian, for example, a population riddled with AIDS. I pointed out to my driver that this was not the first slap inflicted by Uncle Sam on the unfortunate half-island once known as the Pearl of the Antilles. Immediately after the declaration of Haitian independence in 1804, the US cut off all diplomatic and commercial relations with the first Black republic. And though Washington ended up resuming its economic ties, it did not recognize the legitimacy of the

Port-au-Prince government until the second half of the nineteenth century. And the American military occupation of Haiti from 1915 to 1936 did significant damage, as did the support offered by Washington to the dictator Papa Doc Duvalier, then to his son Baby Doc, with the excuse that the Duvaliers offered a guarantee against the development of a left-wing regime in Haiti like Castro's in Cuba.

Trump's comments were disgraceful and full of contempt, but my driver and I both knew that Haitians, be they back home or scattered through the diaspora, are not very charitable toward the tragic half of their island; no one and nobody can prevent criticism of its many shortcomings and failures. There is no end to them, after all. But, of course, there is the way the criticism is spoken, and its intention. My driver and I remembered an exchange dating back to the fall of 2016 about a number of his colleagues who would have voted for Trump rather than the alternative the Democrats were offering. On one hand, the Devil's advocate could counter, wasn't Trump's open racism, a caricature in itself, preferable to the alleged perfidious nature of the Clintons, whose Foundation is looked on with suspicion in Haiti? What about the stagnation of the minimum wage paid to those who work for American multinationals in Haiti? And what about the election of the infamous pop singer Michel Martelly, AKA "Sweet Micky," as president of the country? According to much of the Haitian intelligentsia, both events were tied to Hilary Clinton's backroom dealings when she was Secretary of State.

In light of our past discussions and our shared opinions about the difficult situation of our half of the island with its disasters, natural and man-made, I waited for the 64-thousand-dollar question...

"M'sieur Péan, you are a writer, a journalist, an intellectual. What hope is there for Haiti?"

Writer, journalist, intellectual—all that I accept. But I don't have a crystal ball. I remembered old Délira Délivrance who opens Jacques Roumain's great work of Haitian literature, *Masters of the Dew*, with these seemingly desperate words: "We will all die."

Unfortunately, I could not find such a concise and accurate answer in the fifteen minutes it took the taxi to travel from the CBC building to my house.

★

The "Libérez la parole" festival in which several Quebec writers had participated was ending, and I began the second and final week of my stay in Haiti. I would be spending these well-deserved days of vacation with my friend David, eager to see Cap-Haïtien, a place he had visited some forty years earlier, and my teenaged daughter Laura, who had dreamed of discovering the land of her father's ancestors ever since she was a girl.

The day was endless, and that was partially my fault. Since I had not bought our tickets or reserved our seats on the bus to Haiti's former capital, the fact that we arrived at the Sans Souci agency forty-five minutes before the nine o'clock departure changed nothing. We had to wait for the next bus at eleven o'clock, which irritated me a little, but that's travelling.

As it heads out of Port-au-Prince, the Nationale 1 highway sticks close to the sea. Towns and villages parade past, and their names sound like the fragments of a poem being written: Titanyen, Cabaret, Arcahaie, Justin, Pierre Payen... Not to mention Montrouis, my famous beach of dreams, the setting for one of my first short stories. Between here and the Kingdom of the North, Cap-Haïtien – Cape Haitian to the Americans – the landscape takes on many faces, from the luxuriant jungles of the south, the bare hills that conjure up the deserts of the Westerns that my mother Lady I. so enjoyed, the swampy rice paddies, and much more. Soon we travelled through Saint-Marc, the resort town my father Mèt Mo loved. Luckily, I had remembered to make sandwiches, since Laura was dying of hunger.

After a series of short ones to let passengers off at tiny crossroads communities, our trip included a longer stop at Gonaïves. Our bus entered the Sans Souci station here in the land of the Emperor Dessalines. Everyone got off to have a snack, visit the toilet, stretch their legs, or simply give their ears a welcome respite from the racket of the non-stop *konpa* music the driver insisted on playing at top volume, since who needs silence in this life?

Then everyone took their places again, those who were heading for the heroic northern city, the domain of King Christophe. We reached it at 5:40 p.m., much later than scheduled, if I can use that word. The Sans Souci station lies at the entrance to Cap-Haïtien, and we would need a taxi to reach the Hôtel Beau Rivage where I had reserved rooms for David, Laura, and me. After I put a stop to the childish quarrel between two drivers over who would have the privilege of our fare, I stopped at the counter to make sure we would have seats on the return bus.

The chosen driver introduced himself: Sauveur – yes, "Saviour" – one of those colourful names that Haitians were born to wear. His beat-up jalopy would probably get us to the Beau Rivage. Sauveur was simpatico, though he scarcely made a living driving a taxi, and not from lack of experience. He was courteous enough to use the direct route instead of taking all sorts of detours to take advantage of us tourists. Better yet, he quickly turned into a guide and added no end of explanations and anecdotes about the sites, institutions, and historical monuments we passed along the way: the Tropicana Night Club discotheque, the campus of the Université Anténor Firmin, the Hôtel Impérial, the Cluny market. Awash in information, Laura was thrilled. Maybe her desire to discover the town where her father's family came from would be sated even before we reached our destination.

I was happy with this hurry-up course in the history of the city, too, since I was not completely sure where I was. I had visited Cap-Haïtien only twice, in 1975 on my first family vacation in the country, and in 1988 for the shoot of *Carnets d'un black en Ayiti*, Pierre Bastien's film. The road we travelled was in sad shape. The women vendors walked their usual circuit. From the Sainte-Philomène crossroads, at the southern end of the city, all the way to its centre, garbage of every kind blotted out the landscape. Mixed in with diesel smoke, the terrific stink polluted the atmosphere. What a sad spectacle in the city where King Christophe once reigned! As in certain areas of Port-au-Prince, the mess was among the public health disasters.

Proud as he was of his home like any *nèg okap*, or home-grown Cap-Haïtien citizen, Sauveur did not just tell us the ins and outs of its history. Navigating through the dense traffic, astonishing for such a small city, among the motorcycle taxis and collective *tap-tap* trucks with their bright colours and designs, he wanted to know about us, where we lived, why we had come here. The conversation was lively, and Sauveur proved to be a good guide and a capable driver. Located on the boulevard Carenage, a few minutes from the old town, the Beau Rivage faced the bay. Sauveur helped us carry our bags to the front desk, and I paid the fare, plus a generous tip. And since he was worried about how we would return to the bus station for the trip back to Port-au-Prince, he offered to come and pick us up at the time we desired. He gave me a slip of paper with his phone number. I put the paper in my wallet. No doubt about it, we would call our Saviour.

For a moment there, the young woman at the reception desk had me wondering about the efficiency of my internet travel agency. She had no trace of our reservation. Still, everything was soon settled, and David, Laura, and I would be on time for drinks on Street 14 with Aunt Eva, my father's sister, and my uncle Charles Manigat.

The next day, at the end of the afternoon, the timid young receptionist got up her courage and remarked, "You know, you remind me of someone I knew."

"Really? Who is that?"

Since we were not in Quebec, there was no chance I would be served up the old refrain whereby all Haitian writers are Dany Laferrière.

"You look like Marc Péan," she said.

I nodded. She was not the first person who had pointed out that I looked like my father's brother, the historian of

Cap-Haïtien who wrote such works as *L'Illusion héroïque* and *L'Échec du firminisme*.

"That's very possible. Marc Péan was my uncle."

"Well, he was my grandfather!"

More than a little surprised, I stared at this frail young woman. "My name is Amanda," she added, "and I'm Henri Péan's daughter."

I was too dumbfounded — and tired — to remember whether Marc had a son named Henri. And there was a very good reason. In my family, because hair grew very late on the baby's head, for many years we called my cousin Yul, in honour of Yul Brynner. My cousin's daughter, met by chance in a hotel reserved over the internet: a co-incidence worthy of an O. Henry story!

After the kisses on the cheek that the circumstances demanded, I went to the upstairs deck where David and Laura were waiting, laughing softly to myself.

Since all good things must come to an end, apparently, after several days wandering the streets of the old capital in search of half-faded memories, and visiting aunts, uncles, and cousins who still lived in the cradle of the Péan clan, we had to return to Port-au-Prince to take our plane back to Montreal two days later.

Our last breakfast at the Beau Rivage, an emotional goodbye to young Amanda, and we settled our bill for our stay.

"Do you still have Sauveur's number?" David asked me.

I hunted through my wallet, in vain. The slip of paper

the driver gave me was unfindable.

"You lost it!" my daughter lamented.

"I knew I should have kept it," David grumbled.

Sadly, I had no choice but to ask the receptionist to call a taxi, whose driver could never replace our Sauveur, to whom we had gotten attached. Years later, Laura and David are still a little mad at me.

★

From the Bagotville airport in the Saguenay to the conference centre is a good twenty-minute trip. Luckily, the ride is a lot more pleasant now that the highway that had been promised to the locals for all eternity has finally been completed. If I reached the hotel by five o'clock, I'd have plenty of time to rest up in my room before my duties at the book fair began. This year, I was the guest of honour and would be officiating at the opening.

Could it be that, this year, no one will mistake me for my friend Laferrière?

"You must be Stanley Péan, I bet," the cab driver said over his shoulder. "You haven't been here for a while."

"But I come here once a year at least, usually for the book fair."

"Maybe so. I don't get there myself every time. I'm sure I played baseball with you, but you look a lot younger than I thought."

"If you played baseball, it was with my brother Steve. He's the athlete of the family."

"And you're the intellectual, like your father the teacher."

He couldn't have put it better. Despite the loving war we waged during my teenage years, we always had literature as a common ground and a shared subject. I remember with great fondness the Sunday afternoons we spent together in front of the old black and white television set in the basement, watching with pleasure as the Frenchman Bernard Pivot and his guests graced the set of *Apostrophes*.

"Did you know my father? You're not mixing him up with my uncle Émile?"

"No, no, I'm sure it was him, your father. He taught me French at Guillaume-Tremblay at the end of the 1960s. Your uncle taught math, I remember, and I never had him as a teacher. But you weren't even born back then, I bet."

"Oh, I was on this earth, but I wasn't very old. My younger brother is the only one who was born here, in the Jonquière hospital."

The Jonquière hospital that stands on the boulevard that was once called Centenaire, next to the school I attended for my first three years and the church where I received the usual Catholic sacraments.

"How are your parents? Are they still in the area?"

"My father died in 1987. My mother moved to Quebec City, and she joined him in 2016."

"I'm sorry. I didn't know that. I should have…"

"No harm done. You couldn't have known."

Silence settled over us. The hotel wasn't far now, and its trademark tower would soon be coming into view. I always marvel at the absurdity of it all. My home town of Jonquière, which has since been absorbed into the larger agglomeration of Saguenay, is to my knowledge the only place in the world that has a conference centre right in the middle of nowhere, far from downtown, between a wide cow pasture and a highway.

"Your father was really a great man. Educated like that, there aren't any more like him. He'd quote Jean Racine every other sentence. I'm glad I knew him."

A great man, indeed. At the Jonquière hospital, in his sickroom, Mèt Mo loved to introduce me to his colleagues who gathered around his bedside. He called me his writer son, though I had published no more than a few short stories in obscure little magazines. The sensitive connoisseur of classical French literature that my father was had no admiration for my beginning stories in the science fiction and fantastic style, but he hadn't lost hope that one day he would live to see me write and publish "real" books.

The conference centre appeared. The driver and I exchanged a few final polite greetings. He promised to come by the book fair over the weekend and say hello. He was welcome to; I'd be there every day. I paid and slipped the change and receipt into my pocket, stepped out, and grabbed my bag.

I had reached my destination. End of the line.

Until the next ride.